Jack Clan...

"Are you ca...

"That's right. To a sh...

"You mean a walkdown."

Mallory crossed her arms and gave him a defiant look even though she knew he was right. The famous western cliché where two men met in the middle of the street ready to shoot it out while frightened townspeople ran for cover was called a walkdown.

"I think it's time we settled this," Jack continued.

"Name the time and the place."

"Six o'clock in front of The Bird Cage." He turned away, then glanced back. "Once we set your facts straight, I'll buy you dinner. Never let it be said I'm a gloating winner."

"Never let it be said I'm a loser—of any kind." Mallory Earp's voice was flippant, but an adventurous spirit was running through her, making her reckless. "I'll meet you there."

Dear Reader,

What fun to write a modern-day twist to the old Earp/Clanton feud for which Tombstone, Arizona, is so famous. I got the idea for this book on a visit to that southeastern Arizona town a couple of years ago. I'm lucky enough to live in the same area with some Earps, who kindly let me borrow their family history, and I met some members of the Clanton family who were willing to answer my questions. With resources like those, I knew the story of Mallory and Jack would be worth writing.

I hope you enjoy this trip to the "town too tough to die"!

Sincerely,

Patricia Knoll

Clanton's Woman
Patricia Knoll

Harlequin Books

TORONTO • NEW YORK • LONDON
AMSTERDAM • PARIS • SYDNEY • HAMBURG
STOCKHOLM • ATHENS • TOKYO • MILAN
MADRID • WARSAW • BUDAPEST • AUCKLAND

ISBN 0-373-03402-4

CLANTON'S WOMAN

First North American Publication 1996.

Copyright © 1996 by Patricia Knoll.

Printed in U.S.A.

CHAPTER ONE

THE deserted streets and sidewalks of Tombstone, Arizona were a good place for a showdown.

Mallory Earp stood on the weathered sidewalk planks in front of the O.K. Corral and looked up and down the almost empty street. Since it was early evening, the shops were closed and there were few people about. Most of the town's citizens had been driven indoors by the gathering darkness and the threat of rain.

Masses of gray clouds were banked behind the Dragoon Mountains, swirling sullenly against the last rays of sunset and stabbed with blades of lightning.

The threatening elements didn't bother her. Her mind was fixed on one purpose—finding the man named Jack Clayton. He had been ducking her. She *knew* he had. She had been tracking him for two days. At last, she had him cornered.

Mallory pulled her hat low over her eyes, hitched up her belt, and stepped off the sidewalk. Her boot heels thumped on the pavement as she crossed Allen Street, then crunched gravel when she took a detour down an alley.

It irritated her that it had taken her so long to find him. She didn't have that kind of time to waste. When a full day of phone calls from Tucson had received no personal response, she had come to

Tombstone. In "the town too tough to die", she had asked around. Receiving numerous vague answers had nearly driven her batty. She had finally resorted to walking into a shop and buying twenty dollars' worth of pottery she didn't need in order to pump the woman at the cash register. That's where she'd finally had a break. She had discovered that Jack had been seen in town. She'd had enough of his dodging and weaving, of his unanswered phone calls.

He could run, but he couldn't hide.

Eyes narrowed in concentration, she strode down the alley where she had been directed to look for a small building whose siding was weathered to a silvery gray. Spotting it shouldn't be hard in this well-kept town whose citizens worked hard to keep up appearances in order to attract tourists.

The very word "alley" would have made her pause cautiously in Tucson where alleys were more likely to be dumping grounds or hangouts than thoroughfares for foot traffic. But in this small town, it was a respectable graveled walkway. The path was strewn with rocks and dotted here and there with tiny yellow flowers that grew close to the ground and blossomed at the slightest hint of rain. At last, she spied the building; small and undistinguished, it looked as if a strong wind could pick it up and shift it to the Mexican border. There were windows on each side of its sagging front door. The shades were tightly drawn, but light leaked around the edges. Mallory studied it for a second, wondering what kind of man spent time in such a building and what he did there.

She walked up the two shallow steps to the front door, grasped the knob firmly, and took a moment to square her shoulders and lift her chin. She rapped her knuckles on the door, then checked them for splinters. When she heard a shouted invitation to enter, she pushed the door open and slammed into a wall of cigar smoke.

Her lungs seized up as if a giant hand was squeezing them. Her eyes began to water instantly, and she choked and coughed.

"Shut the door," a man's voice boomed. "You're letting the fresh air in."

She squinted through the gray cloud and wheezed, "That's the idea."

"Not *our* idea," the voice answered. "Shut the door."

Grimacing, Mallory ducked her head outside for one more chestful of oxygen, then walked inside and slammed the door.

Having lost the advantage of surprise, she struggled for a minute between impending asphyxiation and the immediacy of her problem.

She decided to chance suffocation. She'd come this far. She wasn't about to be stopped by the mere fact that she felt as if someone had stuffed her into a bell jar and sucked out all the air. Her stomach was roiling, and she checked to see if her fingernails were turning blue. Even if they had been, she would have gone ahead. For too long, she had let her courage be undermined.

Mallory peered through the haze and spied four men sitting around a square table playing cards. As she walked toward them, she noted the rest of the room. It was as nondescript as the outside. Except for the card table and a table littered with beer cans, there was very little furniture.

The place had scuffed gray linoleum on the floor and faded cabbage rose wallpaper probably slapped on the walls a century ago. This place must have been one of the first buildings in Tombstone, built when lumber had to be hauled in from the railhead in Benson. No doubt, the door at the back of the room led out to a two-holer.

When she stopped beside the table, none of the men looked up. They were busy studying the cards in their hands. They laid down cards and asked for more, threw poker chips into the pile in the center of the table, and generally ignored her. Pointedly, Mallory cleared her throat.

"Just set 'em on the table over there," the man who seemed to be the leader said without looking up.

Mallory glanced around in confusion. "Set *what* on the table?"

That gained her their attention. Heads lifted and four pairs of eyes focused on her over the tips of four glowing cigars. They emitted identical puffs of smoke and exchanged glances.

"You're not bringing more beer from Charlie's Bar," the first man said. He removed the cigar from his mouth, set it in an ashtray by his elbow, and waved away the dense fog in order to see her better.

She knew exactly what he saw—a tall woman in her twenties, too skinny for her own good. Beneath her floaty gauze skirt, she was wearing calf-high boots that gave her even more height and a gold sweater hitched up by a turquoise-studded belt. Her hair was chocolate brown drawn back into a braid that hung nearly to her waist, and topped by a flat straw hat with a brim turned up all around. Purposely, she looked very California casual.

She was striking rather than pretty; her brown eyes were too large and her cheekbones too pronounced. She'd always thought her mouth was too full, the bottom lip enough fuller than the top one that it appeared to pout. If this man didn't stop examining her, she would do more than pout. She would probably say something she would regret.

Mallory whipped off her Helen Kaminski hat and used it as a fan to wave away the cigar smoke as she gave him back look for look.

Even sitting, he was taller and broader of shoulder than the other three men at the table, although that was no proof that he was the builder she was looking for. He was wearing a white Western-style shirt rolled up at the cuffs and had its silver snaps open at the throat. His hair was black, the shade she thought was reserved for a raven's wing, short around his face and curling to his collar in back. It was carelessly tousled as if he had run his fingers through it while puzzling over his hand of cards. His face was square jawed and shadowed with a couple days' growth of beard. His features were strong and lean, serving as a frame for his eyes. They were a startling shade of light green, rimmed with dark gray. Focused on her, they were full of humor.

"No, you're definitely not from Charlie's Bar," he drawled, picking up the conversation as if they hadn't spent a full minute staring at each other. Two of the other men chuckled, catching Mallory's attention. They were about his age, but with dark complexions and even darker eyes. One had a full beard and a gallery of tattoos on his forearms. The other man had a shaved head.

Nerves sent her stomach fluttering. Good grief, what had she stumbled into? Her mind skittered around for the principles of the self-defense classes she had taken.

"Not unless old Charlie's waitresses have suddenly gotten a lot younger and a whole lot prettier," the fourth man said.

Mallory glanced at the speaker. He was older, with gray hair and a handlebar mustache. Even as he spoke, he stood, laid his cards facedown on the table and reached to take his hat from a rack affixed to the wall. "Boys, I've got to go. My wife's waiting supper on me and I promised I wouldn't be late."

His companions protested that he was henpecked, that he was breaking up the game, but he just tipped his hat to Mallory and sauntered out.

"Old Dan doesn't know when he's got it good," the bald one grumbled, reaching over to pick up Dan's discarded cards. He considered them for a second, shrugged, and tossed them back on the table.

The broad-shouldered one who had been doing most of the talking grinned and said, "Oh, yes he does. You should taste his wife's cooking."

His friends chuckled in a friendly way and Mallory's nerves calmed down. Perhaps she had nothing to fear from these men, but she felt that she had been patient long enough. She cleared her throat and faced the green-eyed man. "Excuse me," she said. "I'm looking for Jack Clayton. I was told I could find him here."

The three men exchanged glances. "Jack Clayton?"

"That's right."

The green-eyed one asked, "Why?"

"You're Jack?"

He tilted his head from side to side, indicating the men to his right and left. "And so's he, and so's he."

She blinked. "You're all three named Jack?"

"In a manner of speaking." He shrugged. "Depends on which one of us you want."

Mallory crossed her arms at her waist and stared at him. She'd had enough game playing. "I want the one who's an expert on renovating and rebuilding adobe homes."

"I won't ask the obvious question about why you want him. You must have a home that needs renovating. What's your name?"

"Mallory Earp. I've left messages with your, or your, or your office several times," she said testily, looking at each man in turn.

The spokesman seemed to ignore her tone of voice. He sat forward and regarded her with new interest lighting his eyes. "Did you say Earp?"

"Yes." She lifted her hand, palm out. "And you can forego all the usual jokes about an Earp moving back to Tombstone, returning to the scene of the crime, and so on. I've heard them all. From the

reactions I've had from some people, I imagine the
Clantons and McLowerys would be welcomed with
open arms.''

The two men glanced quickly at their leader, who
grinned at her. ''Yes, ma'am, I bet they would, but
if you received any negative comments, they must
have been from strangers. The natives around here
would welcome an Earp. For the novelty, if for no
other reason.''

He said it as if he relished the idea, and Mallory
didn't know how to react. ''Oh, well, I...'' she
fumbled.

He stood and strode around the table. ''You'll
have to excuse our manners, Miss Earp. It is miss,
isn't it? We should have offered you a chair.''
Smoothly, he drew out the one that Dan had va-
cated. ''Although, the truth is, we have no excuse,
except that these two never learned all their mother
tried to teach them, and I was born in a barn.''

Warily, Mallory looked at him as she moved to
the chair. What was he up to? His eyes were posi-
tively sparkling with devilry. She didn't feel
threatened, only off balance. ''I...uh...thank
you.'' Abruptly, she sat.

''Boys, why don't we put out these cigars? I'm
sure the lady doesn't want to have to smell them.
And I'll open the doors, let some air in here.''

Dutifully, the other men at the table joined him
in stubbing out their cigars, but they gave him
strange looks as he sauntered around throwing both
doors open. A fresh breeze gusted through the room
and they scrambled to pick up the cards. Within
seconds, the smoke began to dissipate from the at-

mosphere, and he returned to the table. As he sat down across from her, the smile he displayed could only be described as self-satisfied.

Mallory blinked at him. "Thank you, Mr. . . . ?"

"Jack's good enough."

"So you *are* the man I'm looking for," she pounced.

"Or he is, or he is."

The one with the full beard nodded at her. "You can call me Jim."

"Why would I call you Jim if your name's Jack?"

"For variety?" He smiled and Mallory completely forgot about her nervousness. He might look like a biker, but he had a sweet smile.

"I'm his brother," the bald one said. "You can call me Fred."

Mallory tucked her tongue into her cheek. "But is that your name?"

"It's what people call me when they don't call me Jack."

She folded her hands on top of the table and looked at them. "Do you three get a lot of mileage out of this routine?"

"Yeah, the ladies seem to like this act," Jack said. "It keeps them guessing." He spread his hands to indicate the cards and chips on the table. "So, how about a little poker?"

Mallory closed her eyes briefly and shook her head. This was making her light-headed. "No, thanks, I'm here strictly on business and I'd like to get it over as quickly as possible. Now, if you'll just tell me which of you runs Cochise Construction, I can take care of my business and be on my way.''

Jack cut the deck, fanned the cards, flipped the edges together, then cut it again, all in a dazzling two seconds. "I never mix business and poker."

"Is this what you've been doing for the past two days that I've been calling?"

His look was swift and mocking. "Maybe it wasn't me you were calling. Play a hand or two with us and then we'll tell you which of us you need to talk to."

Mallory's full lips pulled together grimly. For the past year, she had become accustomed to being on her own, doing what needed to be done. Being assertive was a lesson she had only recently learned, but she was learning it.

However, she had lived in Arizona for ten years and knew a strong streak of stubbornness ran through many of the natives. It had something to do with the fact that Arizona, especially the southeast corner, had been the last real outpost of the Old West. In spite of that stubbornness, she struggled on. "I'm not much of a poker player."

"A relative of Wyatt, Virgil and Morgan who can't play poker? You've got to be kidding," Jack said. "They were three of the biggest cardsharps in the Old West."

Mallory sat up straight. "Now wait a minute. I'm not here to—"

"We'll teach you anything you need to know," he went on. "Fred, deal the cards."

As Fred began to parcel the cards around the table, she scowled and settled back into her chair. "I'm here on business, and—"

"Yeah, we heard you the first time. It'll be taken care of as soon as we finish this hand." He picked up the cards he'd been dealt, glanced at them, then looked at Mallory over the edges. "Unless you're afraid...?"

He left it hanging as a question between them. She didn't even know this man and yet he'd figured out she couldn't back down from a dare. And, darn it, she had spent two days tracking him and wasn't going to leave without the answer she wanted.

With her eyes steady on his, Mallory jerked the sleeves of her sweater almost up to her elbows and slapped her hand down on the five cards before her. She slid them to the edge of the table and picked them up, holding them close to her chest. She peeked at them and was pleasantly surprised. "Well, maybe I do know a little bit about poker."

"Blood tells," Jack observed, studying his own cards. "We'll go easy on you. At first."

"Big of you."

The four of them looked their hands over, traded in some cards, and received more from the dealer. Plastic poker chips rattled together while Mallory tried to figure out how this had come about. All she had done was try to locate someone who could do the needed repairs and renovations on the house she wanted to buy. The only name the realtor had given her was Cochise Construction, based in Benson and supposed to be the best around. She had left endless messages with a gum-popping young secretary, who had assured her that Jack, the owner, would get back to her. Finally, the girl had said he was in Tombstone for the day and would call Mallory as soon as he returned. Apparently, he'd never returned because Mallory had received no phone call, so she had headed for Tombstone to hunt for him. Now, she was sitting at a table, playing poker with him, and she didn't even know which man he was.

"I don't suppose we're playing for money, are we?" she asked innocently, rearranging the cards in her hand and giving the poker chips a meaningful glance.

Jack looked at Jim and Fred, who grinned. He tipped his chair back and watched her. "You think you've got something in that hand worth betting over?"

Mallory knew her face gave away too much. She fought to keep her expression bland. "Maybe."

"Then again, maybe not." He laid his cards down. "Can you beat this, lady and gentlemen? Three of a kind."

Jim and Fred threw their cards down with expressions of disgust.

"How about you, Miss Earp?"

Was that condescension she detected in his voice? Just a hint of assurance that he'd beaten her? She gave a helpless little shrug. "I don't know. Let's see what these three guys think." She laid down three kings and two fives.

"Full house," Jim said, chuckling. "Maybe we *should* be playing for money, Jack. I'd love to see you lose."

Jack regarded her with challenge in his eyes and said, "I think you're right, Jim. I may have outsmarted myself this time."

Mallory looked into his eyes and smiled sweetly. "That's not too difficult, I imagine."

Jim and Fred hooted with laughter and Fred dealt more cards. Jack watched her for a few seconds with a hint of a grin tilting up the corner of his mouth. That look gave Mallory a rush of excitement and made her forget temporarily that she intended to give him a piece of her mind if he was indeed the man she'd been hunting.

They played another hand. This time when Mallory spread a straight flush on the table, Jim and Fred threw their cards down and shuffled to their feet. "Even if you don't, we know how to quit while we're ahead. For someone who doesn't know much about poker, she's winning pretty good," Fred said. "Jack, I think you've found someone better than you."

"Like I said, blood tells," Jack answered mildly.

"Miss Earp, it was nice to meet you," Jim said as he and his brother plucked their cowboy hats from the rack on the wall. "Welcome to Tombstone. Maybe we'll see you again, although I don't think we'll want to play poker with you. It's bad enough losing to Jack." They tipped their hats to her and left, calling out to Jack that they would stop by Charlie's Bar and cancel those beers.

Mallory's lips twisted in a wry smile. Little did Jim know that luck at poker was the only good luck she ever had. Maybe Jack was right. There might be something to the Earp mystique at cards.

It was now fully dark outside and Mallory knew she should have felt nervous about being alone with this stranger, but she didn't feel threatened. Perhaps it was due to the rush of adrenaline she was experiencing because she had bested him at poker.

He must be the man she was looking for. Fred and Jim seemed nice enough despite their fearsome looks, but she doubted they owned the construction business. They simply seemed too easygoing. Jack was obviously the leader.

Jack shoved his chair back and began gathering cards and chips, placing them carefully inside a velvet-lined box.

While he was doing that, Mallory stood and took a turn around the room. She inspected the black window shades that she knew must be years older even than she was. "What is this, some kind of clubhouse?"

He glanced up from where his sure, quick hands were slotting chips into their box. "Nah, just a building I own. Fred and Jim, the Jackman boys who just left, work for me. Whenever we finish a job, we buy a few beers and come here to celebrate."

"Very clever the way you tricked me into thinking they might be the ones I was looking for."

"Hey, can I help it if people call 'em Jack's boys?" He closed the lid with a snap and began emptying ashtrays and beer cans into a garbage bag, which he deposited outside the back door before he locked it.

"You *are* the man I've been looking for, aren't you?" she said, clapping her hands onto her slim hips in irritation.

"I guess I am," he answered, strolling toward her.

"Why didn't you tell me that in the first place?"

Again, a devilish light flickered in his eyes. "I'd never played poker with one of the Earps before. I couldn't pass up the opportunity."

Something in the way he said it and the way he was looking at her had her nerves jumping once again. To hide it, she lifted her chin. "That's a poor reason for wasting my time."

"What are you complaining about? You won."

Mallory drew in a slow, even breath, reminding herself that she needed something from this man and it wouldn't do to offend him. "Can we talk business now?"

He looked straight into her eyes as if he knew what she was thinking, as if he could witness her struggle. "Sure. My secretary, who is also my niece Rhonda, said a lady was looking for me. If I'd known it was urgent, I'd have called you right back."

Mallory relaxed. "Not urgent, but certainly important. I told her that."

"Rhon's a good kid, but I don't think her heart's in her job."

She gave him an incredulous look. "And you let her run your office? Aren't you afraid of losing work?"

His shoulders hitched up briefly, nonchalantly. "Not really. I'm the only one who does what I do. People pretty much have to hire me."

"Sounds like you need some competition."

"Wouldn't matter if I had it. I'd still be the best at what I do."

Mallory gaped at him. He would have sounded arrogant if not for the matter-of-fact tone of his voice. From everything she'd heard, what he said was true, but she hadn't expected to hear him say it outright. She didn't know what to think of him.

He went on. "Where's the place you want renovated?"

"It's...it's on that mesa overlooking the Courthouse Museum. It was owned by a couple named Aylesworth. Maybe you know them. I understand their daughter moved them to California to live with her, and..." Her voice trailed off as he snapped to attention and stared at her.

"The hell you say."

"No, I..." She blinked at him. "What's the matter?"

He moved closer and his chin thrust out. "I've been trying to buy that place for two years. How did you get it?"

Mallory was scrambling to keep up with the unexpected turn this conversation had taken. "I, uh, made an offer, and it was accepted."

"Because she knew it wasn't from me."

"She?"

"Diane Aylesworth. The daughter." He scowled. "She'd rather sell it to anybody but me."

Mallory didn't like the tone of his voice. "I'm not just anybody," she began tartly. "I made a decent offer, and—"

"How much?"

"I beg your pardon?"

"How much did you offer for the place?"

When she told him, he glowered at her. "Mine was more. I knew the woman was vindictive," he said, shaking his head. "But I didn't know how vindictive."

"Why would she...?"

"Let's just say the two of us had a difference of opinion. The Aylesworths lived in the house for a long time, but my grandfather, also named Jack, built it. I wanted to get it back into the family."

Mallory stared at him, at a loss about what to say.

"I'll buy it from you," he said abruptly.

"It's not for sale. I like the house and so does my sister." Which wasn't strictly true. Sammi liked the location and the big lot, but had been appalled at the water stains on the ceiling and the crumbling adobe wall in the living room.

"There are other places around, and—"

She crossed her arms. "It took me ages to find this one and I'm not selling it."

"You Earps sure have a way of moving right in and taking over, don't you?"

Mallory bit her lip to keep from snapping out a reply. She needed this man's help. "Shall we leave my family out of this?"

"I don't know that we can," he muttered.

"Does this mean you won't take the job?"

Jack rubbed his thumb across his jaw as he considered her. "Nah, I guess I can work for an Earp— even one who bought my house when I wasn't looking. Besides, if I do the repairs, I'll at least know they've been done right."

But he wouldn't be too happy about it. Maybe she was making a mistake in hiring him, but there was no one else who was as highly recommended. "Oh, well...good. When can you give me an estimate?"

"Tomorrow. When's a good time?"

Now that he had begun to talk business, Mallory hesitated. His questioning look spurred her on. "My sister and I will be at the house tomorrow afternoon. Come by then."

He nodded, reaching for his cowboy hat and handing her straw hat to her. "I'll walk you to your car."

"That isn't necessary. I can find—"

"I'll walk you to your car."

His tone brooked no argument, so Mallory turned, her full skirt swinging around her legs. "All right. Thank you, Mr. Clayton." Her tone was as ungracious as his. She walked down the shallow steps and made a point of waiting for him, the toe of her boot tap-tapping impatiently.

He took another quick look around to make sure all was secure, then flipped off the lights before joining her at the front where a porch light burned. In its glow, she saw the flash of a pirate's grin, or maybe that of a gunslinger.

"I think you've got my name wrong. It's not Clayton. It's Clanton. Jack Clanton."

CHAPTER TWO

"CLANTON?" Mallory stared at him. "As in . . . Clanton?"

Jack nodded his head, laughter in his eyes. "The very same."

"You could have corrected me sooner," she said, not even bothering to hide her irritation, though it was somewhat self-directed. She had made some uncomplimentary remarks about the Earps' old enemies, the Clantons and McLowerys. How could she have forgotten that in a small town like this, everyone was either descended from, related to, or best friends with everyone else?

"Oh, but that would have ruined the fun." Jack's boots scuffed on the shallow wooden steps as he descended them and came to stand beside her.

Offended, Mallory stiffened and moved away from him, turning toward the alley and the welcoming light of Allen Street beyond. "Excuse me if I don't laugh." She could hear him pause behind her, no doubt surprised by her response. She knew she was overreacting, but old habits die hard.

In his laughter, she heard the mocking tone of her former husband, Charles Garrison. Poking fun at what he termed her naiveté and inexperience had been his favorite pastime. It had taken her a long time to admit that he only did it to make himself seem superior.

Glancing over her shoulder when she passed under a streetlight, she said, "It seems odd to me that none of the people who made cracks about my name happened to mention that there was a Clanton living in town."

"I don't really live here," he said. His tone was easy, but she could see sharp intelligence in his eyes. He was observing her very closely. "I own property in town, but I've got an apartment in Benson."

She came to a full stop and clapped her hands onto her hips. "Can I expect to meet McLowerys around the next corner?"

Jack regarded her for several seconds, his eyes unreadable and his shadowed jaw set. "Not if they get a hint of your welcoming attitude."

Turning, she started off again and he lengthened his strides to catch up to her. In a few seconds, they were on the wooden sidewalk that bordered the paved street.

Mallory squared her shoulders and pushed her hat to the back of her head so it wouldn't prevent her from seeing him clearly. "If you don't like my attitude, you don't have to work for me. I'm sure I can easily find someone else to do the job."

Challenge lit his eyes and Jack stepped up to her so that they were standing toe-to-toe. She was tall, but he was taller, his size swamping her. Mallory knew she should have chosen her words, or her tone, more carefully, but she couldn't back down now. She tilted her head back and held his gaze until she thought her jaw would break.

Jack's voice was low and full of humor at her expense, but it held an underlying edge of iron.

"You can't find anyone else to do the job, easily or any other way. I'm going to do it. I told you, my grandfather built that place and I'm the one who's going to repair it. Maybe I can't own it...yet—but I can damned well make sure it doesn't fall down from neglect and bad repairs before I can get it back into the family."

Incensed, she splayed a hand over her chest. "Excuse me? Are you giving me notice that you plan to put me out of my house?"

He lifted his hands away from his sides and she was momentarily reminded of a gunslinger preparing to draw. "You're not in the house yet, and you won't be until I finish the repairs. I'm just saying that when you're ready to sell, I'll be ready to buy."

Mallory's dark eyes widened and she stared at him, at a loss for words. "Well," she breathed. "You've got your nerve if you think I'll sell—"

"I'm not talking about buying it now," he interrupted with swift impatience. "I know I've lost, but I also know it's only temporary. I want you to understand that I plan to do the work on that place. As far as I'm concerned, we have a deal, and we might as well shake hands on it right now."

He was standing only inches from her, and when he stuck out his hand, the tips of his fingers grazed the front of her sweater, plucking at the knit fabric as if wanting to draw her closer. Unnerved, Mallory stepped back.

She had been married for six years. Six long and painful years. In fact, it was the settlement from her divorce that was enabling her to buy the shop

in Tombstone and a new home for herself and
Sammi.

She wasn't a stranger to men, to the touch of a
man's hand, but she was a stranger to the off-
balance feeling that was causing her to stare cautiously at Jack and his waiting hand.

Beneath the brim of his hat, his eyes glittered at
her, but his outstretched hand remained steady.
"Around here, it's an insult to refuse to shake a
man's hand when you've settled on a deal." His
voice was low and as hard as granite.

Still, Mallory stared at him. The swift change in
him sent surprise and nervous anticipation shooting
through her. Her tawny eyes widened and her
tongue sneaked out to dampen her dry lips. She
had been fooled. Beneath that easygoing exterior
was a ruthless man. He might not be an outlaw like
his forebears, but he was no pushover, either. A
voice inside her cried out that she was giving in too
easily, letting him control her, something she had
sworn wouldn't happen again, but his will compelled her.

"Around here," he went on, "a handshake seals
an agreement or a business deal."

She knew that. She was a businesswoman who
had just purchased her own shop. It wasn't the
agreement she was worried about. Touching him
worried her. Something told her that she would be
handing over far more than the renovation of her
house.

Ridiculous, she decided, and her hand shot out
to grasp his. It was exactly as she had feared. His
big, muscled hand with its callused palm and long

fingers wrapped around hers, nearly swallowing it whole. It felt warm, dry and possessive.

Mallory gave his hand one quick shake and snatched hers away. She stepped back, her boots echoing a rapid beat on the boardwalk. Tilting her head, she tried to appear nonchalant, as if she hadn't just made a complete fool of herself, as if an unaccustomed tingling warmth wasn't still rocketing through her veins.

Jack seemed disconcerted, too. The thoughtful expression on his face told her he was choosing his next words carefully, but he didn't seem any more eager to resume their conversation than she was.

Fortunately, she was saved from having to make further conversation by the arrival of a highly polished black pickup truck. It rolled to a stop beside them, and one of the darkly tinted windows cranked down. Fred Jackman stuck his shiny bald head out.

"Hey, boss, we forgot to ask if you've got any work for us tomorrow. You going to be needing us?"

Jack, who had been staring at Mallory, turned slowly and focused on Fred. Mallory breathed in a deep gulp of air and wished she dared push her hands against her fluttering stomach.

"No, Fred, not tomorrow. Not for a while, in fact. I'll let you know."

"Sure thing. See you." Fred gave Jack a two-fingered salute, then called to Mallory. "Good night again, Miss Earp."

Mallory gave him a weak nod, then straightened abruptly as an idea occurred to her. There must be another reason for Jack's insistence on doing the renovations to her house. He must need the money. He didn't have enough work to keep his employees busy.

She gave him a swift, sideways glance. It was difficult to tell about a man from his outward appearance and impossible to tell if he was successful in life. She had learned two things about Jack already, though.

He was self-assured and determined and it was best to avoid misunderstandings by getting all of her facts straight up front.

"Do you want to do the repairs on my house because you need the money?"

Jack looked at her and frowned. "Sure, I can always use money. Who can't? Why do you ask?"

"You don't have any work for your employees, so you must be desperate for work."

"And you have an amazing ability to jump to conclusions," he answered dryly as he glanced around. "Where did you say your car is parked?"

So much for that idea, she thought with a mental shrug. She could only conclude that he did, indeed, have no other motive for wanting to do the work on her house.

He planned to fix it up so he could take it away from her at the first opportunity.

She had known this man barely an hour, but she had already learned that dealing with him would be straightforward, though not simple.

"Oh, over there," she said with a sigh, indicating a lot at the end of the street. It was high time she stopped butting heads with the man and went on her way. Sammi was alone in their motel room and would be worried about her.

Jack and Mallory walked the half block to her car and he waited until she had unlocked the door and was ready to climb in before he said, "Good night, Mallory. I'll see you tomorrow. I'm looking forward to a long and productive...partnership."

"So am I," she answered coolly, and knew she was lying through her teeth. There was nothing else she could do now, though. She was committed and wished she wasn't.

Quickly, she sat, he closed the door, and she started the engine. As she drove away and made the turn that would take her to the highway, she glanced back to see Jack still standing where she had left him.

He stood with his feet slightly apart and his arms crossed over his chest. He looked as if he owned the world. Mallory had the feeling that if they were partners in any way, she was the junior one.

Her hands gripped the wheel and she had to force herself to relax them as she tried to analyze what bothered her about him. Maybe bothered wasn't the right word, she thought. Intrigued might be more accurate. And that thought disturbed her even more.

Her ancestors may have found the original Clantons and their friends, the McLowerys, to be dangerous, but she doubted that those old-time outlaws had anything on Jack.

He didn't carry a gun. He may never have broken a law, but her reaction to him told her he was dangerous just the same.

*   *   *

"Please tell me you're kidding."

"No, I signed all the papers this morning. This place is ours."

"Oh, joy."

"It'll be perfect for us." Mallory looked around happily at the home she had purchased, then at her sister's dismayed face.

"It doesn't look any better than it did the first time we saw it." Samantha's gentle brown eyes, as soft as a doe's, were full of worry. She was winding a strand of chestnut hair around and around her finger in her lifelong signal of distress.

The two of them were standing on opposite sides of the room, Mallory looking the place over with eager anticipation, Sammi with dread.

"I know, but like I told you, I've found someone who can do repairs. In fact, his grandfather built this place, so he'll do a good job fixing it up just the way we want it." She hoped. After a good night's sleep, she had decided she had been suffering from an overactive imagination last night. There was nothing about Jack Clanton that should unnerve her. Theirs was a simple business deal, and she was the boss.

Mallory had talked to her realtor that morning and mentioned Jack's desire to own the house. The woman had said she'd known about it, but Diane Aylesworth had insisted he couldn't have it. Mallory wondered what on earth he had done to earn Miss Aylesworth's dislike.

"Mallory?"   Sammi's   voice   quavered. "What's wrong?"

Realizing that she had been frowning, Mallory faced Sammi with a manufactured smile. "Nothing. Nothing at all." Long-legged and graceful, her rich brown ponytail swinging down her back like a rope of satin, she strode across the littered wooden floor and put an arm around her petite sister's shoulders. Her eyes were alive with anticipation as she gave Sammi a squeeze. "Ah, don't worry, honey, it's going to be all right. You'll like this house once it's ready, and you'll like it here in Tombstone."

"Why couldn't we stay in Illinois, or in Tucson? Why do we have to move here?"

Repressing an inward sigh because they had been through this a number of times before, Mallory gave her sister a second quick hug, then released her. Shy and quiet, overprotected by their parents because she had been slower than other children, Sammi had always needed constant encouragement and reassurance, now more than ever before.

"Because Mom and Dad waited a long time for their retirement from the hardware store back home and because they deserve a chance to do what they want without having to worry about us."

"Yeah, but I worry about them. They're so far away—building homes for poor people in Africa." Sammi shook her head as if she still couldn't believe it.

"You could have gone along," Mallory pointed out.

Sammi gave her an in-your-dreams look and Mallory grinned. "Well, then, kiddo, you're stuck with me. The gift shop I bought in town is a thriving business where we can work together. You want us to be together, don't you?''

Sammi cast her sister a doubtful look and Mallory burst out laughing. "Well, don't knock me over with your enthusiasm.''

"I've never worked in a shop. I've never worked anywhere.''

"But you can learn. You'll be good with the customers. People always like you.''

"I know.''

Mallory bit her lip to keep from laughing. Sammi was completely without guile. She always said what she thought and got away with it because of her natural sweetness.

She started to offer more reassurances, then thought better of it. At least Sammi was acknowledging that she could deal with customers. That admission indicated some progress. She had been known to do things she didn't really want to do just to please her sister or parents. Mallory didn't want that to happen. It was important that Sammi feel she was really part of the decision without any pressure placed on her.

It was even more important that she begin to grow up. After all, she was eighteen now. She needed to start being responsible for herself and her own decisions.

Getting her to this point had been a real struggle, much of it between Mallory and her parents. They had worked in the family hardware store years after they should have retired and set out on their longed-for Peace Corps service because Sammi didn't want to go along and they couldn't bear to leave her behind.

It had taken a long time for Mallory to convince them, and their agreement had only come about when Mallory had actually filed for divorce. They'd realized that she and Sammi would be good for each other. Because their letters were so full of enthusiasm over their work and the people they were helping, Mallory didn't dare tell them things weren't working out very well. She could only hope Sammi's melancholia would improve with time.

As if she could read Mallory's thoughts, Sammi sighed.

Knowing she needed some space, Mallory, full of her usual restless energy, walked across to the wide windowsill, the only available seating in the bare room. The seat was cracked and the front half of the board rocked beneath her as she sat down. Cautiously, she turned so that her back was to the afternoon sun that streamed in, warming her through her white T-shirt and snug jeans. She stretched her long legs out before her and arched her back to the welcome rays.

"We've had so many changes already," Sammi said softly.

"I know, and I'm sorry about it. Things will never be like they were, though. Even after Mom and Dad come home, they won't be going back to Illinois. They'll buy a house here in Arizona."

"I know." Sammi, as tiny and pale as a waif, circled the big, empty room and gazed into the decrepit kitchen. Mallory had to admit the place did look pretty bad. It wasn't at all like the beautiful home in which they had grown up. That house had been sold and the furnishings put in storage.

With a determined smile, Mallory motioned to her sister. "Come here and look at this view."

Obediently, Sammi crossed the room and Mallory steadied the board so she could join her. They sat knee-to-knee on the wide sill and gazed across the small valley to the mesa below. On it was perched one of the most notorious towns of the Old West.

Mallory had been surprised when she had first seen the town on a day's visit with some college friends several years ago. It was smaller than she had expected it to be, considering that it had once been the most cosmopolitan town between San Antonio and San Diego. There was very little evidence of the silver mines that had once drawn miners from as far away as China and Wales, although a person didn't have to venture very far afield before running into honeycombs of abandoned mine shafts made even more dangerous by flooding from the high underground water table.

Since that first visit, Mallory had kept a special affection for the place. She knew a great deal about the history of the area, in fact, the whole state, thanks to six years with her ex-husband, who was a professor of Western history.

With an effort, she focused on the view. Thoughts of him weren't going to intrude on this beautiful day.

The sweep of desert up to the mesa was beautiful. From where they sat, she could see the redbrick Tombstone Courthouse Museum. Once the courthouse for Cochise County, it was now a state historic park, beautifully preserved and renovated much as it had been one hundred years ago. Far in the distance, she could see the Dragoon Mountains.

She felt as though it would be very easy for her to develop roots here. After the terrible upheavals and emotional storms of the past year, this new start was what she and Sammi both needed. She propped her small, pointed chin in her hand, placed her elbow on her knee, and enjoyed the view.

On top of the mesa, she saw a man on horseback. He cantered down a paved road, then onto a narrow path. She admired the easy sway of his body as he fitted his own rhythm to that of his loping mount. He seemed so much a symbol of the West, of the independence and self-sufficiency she sought for herself and for Sammi, that she sighed dreamily. She watched him until he headed his horse down a trail into the small valley and disappeared behind a stand of mesquite. She turned to her sister eagerly. "We could get you a horse. Would you like that?"

"If it's gentle."

"Nah," Mallory teased. "I thought we'd get you a bucking bronco." When Sammi didn't react but still looked worried, Mallory sighed and said, "We'll like it here. Remember, we grew up in a small town."

"Not this small, and it was only a couple of hours to Chicago."

"If we miss the city too much, Tucson is only an hour away. We can go in for a wild shopping spree anytime you want."

"How about now?"

Ignoring her, Mallory went on enthusiastically. "We've got family history in this town. Our great-great-grandfather's cousins were lawmen here, remember? Wyatt, Virgil, Morgan. Warren and James lived here, too. That practically makes us natives."

"Didn't you tell me that one of them died here?"

Never should have mentioned that. Mallory wrinkled her nose. "Well, yeah. The one named Morgan."

"And another one was shot so bad he could never use his arm again."

"Mind like a steel trap," Mallory muttered. Where was Sammi's usual vagueness and uncertainty now?

"What did you say?"

"I said, too bad about that. The one who was injured was named Virgil. But that's not going to happen to us, and look at this house," she said heartily, waving her hand around. "I've always loved adobe. Walls a foot thick, cool in the summer and warm in the winter. What more could we ask for?"

Sammi eyed the dirty floor. The Mexican tiles should have been a reddish brown but instead were dun-colored. "How about a broom?"

"Now, Sis, it's true that the last owners weren't exactly in love with cleanliness. They were elderly and things were probably too much for them, and—"

"They kept a goat in the bedroom."

Darn that big-mouthed realtor. "That shouldn't bother you, as much as you love animals."

"It *smells* like a goat."

"We'll clean the room."

"There are stains on the kitchen ceiling and the sink has a big crack in it."

Even someone with limited experience in the world knew what that meant—a leaky roof and bad plumbing. "We'll get it fixed." Mallory nodded thoughtfully. "In fact, I think we'll remodel the kitchen. The cabinets are a joke."

"This whole house is a joke," Sammi said, but a tiny smile was beginning to tickle the edge of her mouth.

Mallory encouraged the game with a grin of her own. She reached over and tugged on one of Sammi's curls.

Sammi returned the favor, grabbing Mallory's ponytail and giving it a pull as she said, "Both the bedrooms are tiny, smaller than my closet back home in Illinois."

Mallory spread her hands wide. "We'll turn your whole bedroom *into* a closet and you can sleep outside."

Sammi giggled. "It might be winter by the time we move in here."

"I'll give you a blanket—two on a really cold night," Mallory said magnanimously.

"I think I'd rather sleep inside after all."

"Maybe Jack can make the bedrooms bigger."

"Maybe he can build us a whole new house," Sammi suggested hopefully, but Mallory could tell she was resigning herself to their home.

As she glanced around, Mallory's agile mind began clicking over possibilities. The walls and floors were sound. The thick walls were plastered on the inside, but the paint was dingy and streaked with stains whose origins she didn't want to think about too closely.

Seventy-five years old, with wiring and plumbing that validated its age, the place had charm and character all its own. Sure it was dirty, well, all right, filthy, but it could be cleaned.

This house would be remodeled the way she wanted it. She could help Jack by giving him directions on exactly how she and Sammi wanted it done. She intended to be fully involved in the project.

"You loved this place the minute you saw it," Sammi said with a hint of accusation in her tone.

Roused from her thoughts, Mallory turned back to her sister. "Well, did you see one you liked better?"

"No."

"Then this is it for us."

"I bet it doesn't snow here."

Accustomed to the way Sammi slipped from one topic to another, needing assurance on several points at once, Mallory answered gently. "That makes it all the more special because it's so rare."

Silence stretched between them as Sammi thought things over. Mallory looked away from her sister's struggle. The rider she had noticed earlier had emerged from the arroyo about half a mile away. He cantered easily along the road, his body swaying with the horse's movements.

Sammi's hesitant voice brought her back to their conversation. "I can have animals?"

"All you want. I already checked with the city authorities. It'll be fine as long as they're properly penned up and cared for. I'll bet Jack knows someone who can build the pens for us."

She hesitated, realizing that she sounded very sure of Jack Clanton—strange behavior for someone who was so hesitant to hire him only last night and felt manipulated into doing so.

Mallory pushed that troubling thought aside and focused on Sammi, reading the acceptance in her sister's soft face. "The size of this lot is one of the reasons I like this place so much."

They were both quiet for a moment, deep in their own thoughts, until Sammi said, "Is it going to be all right, Mallory?"

Mallory slipped her hand into Sammi's and gave it a squeeze. "It's going to be perfect."

Sammi rolled her eyes at the exaggeration. "You've got to be kidding."

"Have a little faith in your big sis, will ya?"

They smiled at each other. The phrase was an old family joke. Whenever the three women in his life were giving him grief or questioning his judgment, their father would remind them to have a little faith in their old dad. The memory made Mallory ache for her parents and she knew Sammi felt the same.

"Why don't we see if we can call Mom and Dad this weekend? We can tell them about the house."

"They'll be thrilled," Sammi answered in an ironic tone, but she smiled. "Promise to call them?"

"We can try." Telephone reception was always chancey where their parents were stationed, but occasionally the connection was as clear as a bell. "We might get lucky."

The sound of a horse's hooves striking gravel caught their attention and they turned toward the window. Jack Clanton cantered up the driveway astride a big roan. Mallory straightened in surprise. He was the rider she had been watching. The one she had been admiring. Mallory shook her head, dismayed at the thought even as she noticed the sure way he handled the reins. She had to admit that he looked very handsome and masculine dressed in a blue plaid shirt, denim jacket and jeans. His tan cowboy hat was set squarely above his eyes.

Mallory recalled the strange sensations she had experienced last night when they'd shaken hands on the deal.

Even now, she felt a breathless moment of confusion. She had to get control of this, she berated herself. She took a couple of breaths, then frowned as she concentrated on Jack. Whoever heard of a contractor coming on horseback to estimate a job? Trust Jack Clanton to do things his own way.

"Come on." She clasped her sister's hand and drew her to her feet. "This is the man we've been waiting for."

CHAPTER THREE

WHEN they emerged from the house, Jack pulled up the big roan mare and dismounted. He let the reins dangle to the ground, which allowed the horse to move to a patch of grama grass growing at the corner of the house.

Jack dug a small notebook and a slim calculator from his shirt pocket and strolled over to greet them. "Afternoon, Miss Earp," he said, tipping his hat. In the bright afternoon sunlight, she could see things she hadn't noticed in the artificial light of his little weathered shack or the dimness of the streetlights.

His light green eyes were as sharply intelligent and observant as ever, but now she could see fine lines that rayed out from their corners. They were indications of experience and made her think that this man's life hadn't been easy, but that he had come to terms with it. She found herself focusing on his hands, recalling their touch, their toughness and strength, and unwillingly comparing them to Charles's soft, almost feminine ones.

Heavens, she thought, giving herself a mental shake. She had to stop this!

Her eyes shot up to his. "Hello, Mr. Clanton." She knew her voice sounded stiff, but she couldn't seem to help it. "This is my sister, Samantha. She'll be living here with me."

Sammi held out a fragile hand to Jack, who took it gently in his own. She met his welcoming grin with a shy smile.

Mallory sighed in audible relief that Sammi seemed to accept him so readily, and Jack shot her a swift, questioning glance before looking back at Sammi. "Hello, Samantha. It's nice to meet you. I hope you like Tombstone."

"Me, too," she said in an aggrieved tone that seemed to charm him. She gave his horse a look of longing that held an edge of fearfulness. "What's your horse's name?"

"Garnet," he said, turning to look at the animal. "She was staying with a friend of mine in town. He's got little kids who like to ride her—or torment her, depending on your point of view. I rode her over so she'd get some exercise. Do you like horses?"

"Some of them."

Her tone was dubious enough to make Mallory smile and Jack chuckle. "Why don't you come meet her?" He led the way to the mare, who was munching placidly. Mallory followed close on their heels and hovered as he showed Samantha the area behind Garnet's ears where she liked to be scratched. "You don't have to worry, Samantha. She's as gentle as a baby."

Sammi touched Garnet's shiny mane, then stroked it boldly. When the mare went on munching grass, Sammi grew more confident and looked up with a smile. "I'll stay here with Garnet while you two look at the house." She grimaced. "I've seen it already."

Jack glanced from Sammi to Mallory, who could feel a flush climbing her cheeks. Interested speculation lit his eyes. Mallory was positive she knew what he was thinking—that there was disagreement in the Earp household over their new home. She couldn't deny it; she only hoped he didn't plan to use it to try to persuade her to sell.

"Why don't you lead the way, Mallory?" he asked. "Show me what you want done."

Something in his tone baited her, and darn it, she couldn't resist answering in kind. "Of course. I can show you *exactly* what we want done." Head high, she preceded him into the house, stopping in the middle of the living room and indicating it with a wave of her hand. "Shall we start in here?"

"Sure, that is if you don't want to reconsider selling it to me." He removed his hat and laid it on the window seat, then walked over to one of the walls where a long crack marred the surface. A small mound of adobe dust had spilled from it. He chipped away some of the paint and plaster, then examined the small hole he'd made.

She crossed her arms. "I thought we'd settled this last night. No, I don't want to reconsider."

He gave her a quick sideways glance, then stood to look around.

Troubled, Mallory watched him. Somehow this room seemed smaller with him in it. He disturbed her and it was more than his renewed offer to buy her new home. Looking at the way his competent hands tested the damage to the wall made her lose her focus. She didn't want to be aware of him.

"Why do you want to live in Tombstone?" He moved into one of the bedrooms and she had to follow in order to answer him.

"I bought a business here. It seems to make sense to live near my work."

"I suppose so," he agreed. Catching a whiff of the overwhelming goat smell of the room, he wrinkled his nose. "Whew! Aylesworths weren't too discriminating about the company they kept, were they? I wonder if they're keeping a goat in Diane's condo." The idea seemed to please him.

Mallory crossed her arms over her waist and leaned against the door frame. "Exactly what did you do to get her so mad at you?"

Jack's head came up. "Is that personal interest I hear in your voice?"

"Certainly not," Mallory said automatically, then could have kicked herself for sounding so quickly defensive. "I'm . . . I'm merely wondering if people are usually so vindictive toward you."

Jack's mouth tilted up. "Only the ones who think they can trap me into marriage."

"Are you opposed to marriage?"

He shrugged. "Not at all, but when I'm ready, I intend to be the one doing the asking. How about you?"

Mallory gave him an uncertain look. She wished she'd never brought this up. "How about me . . . what?"

"What are your thoughts on marriage?"

"I've tried it, as a matter of fact, and I think it's fine if you like traps." When he looked as if he was going to ask another question, she straightened away from the door and walked across the stained and scarred floor. She rubbed it with her shoe. "What do you think needs to be done to this floor?"

Jack hesitated for several seconds before answering. Mallory could feel his gaze boring into her for long, breathless seconds. She wondered what he was thinking, wanted desperately to run her suddenly sweaty palms down the front of her jeans and dry them off, realized to her dismay that they had passed the point of employer/employee and strayed into a personal conversation—and it was all her fault.

Finally, he answered, and she let her breath out in slow, silent relief. "It will have to be stripped, treated, and resealed," he went on. "It'll be expensive. Sure you don't want to reconsider?"

This she could deal with. She lifted her chin and gave him a direct look. "Did anyone ever tell you that you sing a one-note song?"

His slashing black brows lifted. "Not lately."

"Trust me, you do." Mallory rolled her eyes up. "Take a look at the ceiling. This floor is the least of my worries."

Jack tilted his head and examined the massive spread of water stains. "Roof damage. More expense." He made a notation in his book, then asked in a studiously casual manner, "So, why do you want to stay?"

He was warning her off, but Mallory would have none of that. This conversation wasn't about renovations. It was about ownership. And they might as well establish ownership right away. "Because I . . . *we* have family history here."

"Your sister doesn't seem to be as crazy about the idea as you are."

"She'll get used to it." Mallory cringed at her own tone as she watched his eyes widen in question. She'd be darned if she was going to be on the defensive. Her decisions about her life, and Sammi's, were none of his business. "She'll like it here. She has a reason to."

If Jack was surprised by her tone, he didn't show it. He gave her a straight-from-beneath-the-eyebrows look and asked, "Is this family history of yours why you chose Tombstone? Hoping to drum up business for your shop by advertising your name?"

"No," she said through her teeth. "I don't plan to capitalize on my name any more than you do on yours. But it's different for you, isn't it?" she asked in a voice that dripped honey. "If you called your business Clanton Construction, you'd have no customers at all. I mean, it would be like advertising dishonesty."

A long moment of silence followed that careless statement. Mallory swallowed hard and waited for his response. She wouldn't blame him if he turned around and stalked out, leaving her to find another contractor to do the work. She couldn't imagine what had possessed her. She *never* talked to anyone that way.

Instead of walking out, he stepped closer. His eyes were full of scorn. "What a wicked tongue you have, Miss Earp. You must do a lot of damage with it."

Mallory cleared her throat. "I'm...I'm, uh, sorry for saying that. It was inexcusable."

Another long, awkward moment followed before Jack nodded in acceptance of her apology, but he didn't move away. Mallory had to tilt her head back to maintain eye contact. She could feel embarrassed color climbing her cheeks. A wise woman would have backed down, stepped away, anything to break that contact.

Mallory questioned her own wisdom when she lifted her chin a notch higher and said, "To answer your question, I chose Tombstone because of its history, the shop and this house. Also, because of its closeness to the Chiricahuas. I'm interested in the history of the area and its legends."

Jack tilted his head, listening with deep interest. In his eyes, she saw a hint of respect and was glad she hadn't backed down.

He nodded. "Those mountains have as many legends as they have peaks."

"I know." Warming to the subject she loved, Mallory forgot their momentary animosity. "I've been fascinated by them ever since I moved to Arizona, especially the one about a bank robber named Lying Jude Bluestone."

"Excuse me?" Jack had snapped to attention and his hands fell to his sides. "Did you say Bluestone?"

At the instant alertness in his face, Mallory said, "I see you've heard of him."

"You could say that."

Mallory paused, expecting him to go on, but when he didn't, she said, "Well, then you know that the story says he robbed the bank in Willcox and a local sheriff went after him. The sheriff returned without the money and without Jude, but he was able to retire comfortably only a few months later. People said he—"

"I know what they said," Jack interrupted in a flat tone. "You shouldn't believe all those old tall tales."

Her back straightened. Once again, she heard the echo of Charles's voice telling her that her opinion didn't count, her thoughts didn't matter, her conclusions were wrong. "There's no proof it's a tall tale."

"There's no proof it isn't," he answered shortly. "Don't tell me you're one of those fools who thinks they can find Jude's treasure?"

"I'm not a fool."

"People have been looking for that money for a hundred years and no one's ever found a trace of it."

"Well, they didn't have what..." It was an effort, but Mallory forced herself to stop.

"You were saying?" he prompted.

"Never mind." Searchers never told all they knew, and especially not to someone as sharply intelligent as Jack. "It's possible that I can find it," she hedged. "Stranger things have happened."

Jack was quiet for a moment as if he planned to pursue the subject, then decided to bide his time. Finally, he said, "Stranger than a Clanton working for an Earp?"

Mallory blinked, then nodded in agreement even as she wondered what he was really thinking. She hadn't known him very long, but she could already tell that he wasn't the type of man who gave up easily. He would return to their discussion of Lying Jude's treasure in his own good time.

She fervently wished she'd kept her mouth shut.

He turned away and began inspecting the room, running his hand over the walls, thumping the baseboards with the toe of his boot. Mallory was impressed with his thoroughness but she wasn't surprised by it. Whether he was working or playing cards, he seemed to be good at whatever he attempted. She thought of his boast the night before that he was the best at his job and decided it was probably true.

As she watched, he examined one of the windows, then grasped the sash to tug it open. Mallory found herself watching the way his muscles strained the seams of his denim jacket and wondering if the snaps in front were going to pop open. The thought had warmth swirling through her. If she moved around in front of him, she could... She managed to stop before she did anything so foolish. Briefly, she closed her eyes and wondered what on earth was happening to her. There was a very strong chance she was losing her mind.

At last, he lifted the window to let the breeze in. "Did you choose Tombstone because of the local history or because of your family history?"

She clasped her hands together at her waist. "Does it matter, Mr. Clanton? Everybody knows the Earps were the good guys." That brought him around to focus on her. The challenging look in them could have stopped a charging rhino, but Mallory had her daring up now. "It's a well-known fact that the Earps were trying to bring some law and order to this town because it was being ravaged by the Clanton and McLowery gang."

His hands lifted to his waist and his head jutted toward her. "If you'll pardon my saying so, that's a bucket of donkey muffins, Miss Earp." Before she could sputter out a reply, he went on, "A well-known fact," he snorted derisively. "I think you need to be educated in the truth."

Her jaw dropped. "The truth?"

"How much do you really know about the feud between the Earps and the Clantons?"

"Enough."

"Meaning nothing."

Mallory held on to her temper by pure force of will. She had only been with him for twenty minutes and she felt as if she had gone ten rounds wrestling a grizzly. This conversation had gone in every possible direction except the one she intended. If she could just get through the next hour or so, she would know how to deal with him. She was beginning to rethink her plan to be involved in the actual work on the place. It would be in her best interest to stay as far away from him as possible.

She started from the room, but looked back over her shoulder at him. "If you're finished in here, there are other rooms to see, unless you're changing your mind about taking on this job."

The determination in his face matched hers. "I wouldn't dream of it."

Walking with quick, sharp steps, Mallory led him to the bedroom that she intended to have for her own. "Arguing over something that happened more than one hundred years ago is perfectly ridiculous."

"Afraid you'll lose?" Jack asked calmly as he sauntered along behind her. "I can't believe a relative of the Earps would run from a fight."

"I'm not exactly a direct descendant. The relationship is a distant one," she said with a toss of her head that sent her braid dancing. She turned to face him. "However, I don't appreciate..." Her words stumbled over themselves and fell flat.

He was regarding her with laughter in his eyes because he had done what he had obviously planned—gotten a rise out of her. He was teasing her and she had immediately gone on the defensive. Since the minute she had met him, she had been energized and challenged more so than at any time in the past year. What was it about this man that sent her into such quick overreactions?

She cleared her throat and said briskly, "We were wondering if there was some way to make these rooms larger. Sammi and I would both like more space."

He lifted an eyebrow at her abrupt change of subject, but he looked around and answered, "The separating wall could be taken out and this made into one big room, and another room could be added on. It'll raise the cost, of course. In fact, it'll almost double it." He punched some buttons on his calculator and wrote them in his notebook.

"I never doubted that for a minute," she said sweetly. "But we can negotiate."

"Something that our ancestors should have learned to do," he said.

"Good point," she answered blandly, refusing to be drawn in again. The dangerous gleam in his eyes made her heart beat in a quick, steady patter of anticipation. Appalled to realize that she was actually enjoying this debate, she said, "Here's the bathroom."

She marched in and stood beside the old-fashioned tub. A narrow shower spigot stood high on the wall above it. She turned the knob with a twist of her wrist. There was a mighty heaving and gurgling before a single drop of water emerged to plop onto the rust-stained porcelain below.

"As you can see, the plumbing needs work."

"I'll get Fred to look at it. He's our plumber."

"Good." She reached to turn off the faucet, but his hand was there before hers.

"Here, I'll do that," he said.

"I don't need your help." She brushed his hand away, looking up when she heard another gurgling rumble from the pipes overhead. Alarmed, she twisted the knob with one hand, and reached up with the other to turn the shower head away. It tilted upward at a crazy angle, but before she could straighten it, a blast of icy water gushed out and hit Jack full in the face.

Yelping, he leaped backward. His arms flew out, clipping Mallory across the shoulder and sending her reeling across the room. She crashed into the opposite wall and had to scramble to regain her balance. Jack grabbed for the faucet handles. He twisted the water off, then began flicking water from his face.

To her horror, Mallory felt a bubble of hysterical laughter trying to escape. She gulped it down frantically and said, "I didn't do that on purpose."

He stopped for a second and his head came up. "If I thought you had, you'd be under that shower right now finding out how cold it really is."

"Oh," was all she could say as he took off his jacket and used it to finish drying his face. She cleared her throat again and he looked up.

"I'm warning you, Miss Earp, you'd better not laugh."

"I wouldn't dream of it," she said heartily. "No, sir, not me. Absolutely not." She ended on a hiccup and looked at him sheepishly. He gave a dry snort that seemed to echo what she was already thinking. This was the strangest business relationship she had ever begun. On the other hand, she'd never met a businessman quite like Jack Clanton.

"Good. Glad to hear you're not laughing." He finished drying off and slung his jacket over his shoulder.

Mallory rocked on her heels and spread her hands wide. "Sooo, I guess it's safe to say that the plumbing does work after all."

"Looks that way," he answered in a disgruntled tone. Jack held up his jacket and shook it, then looked up to meet her eyes, which were bright with suppressed laughter. His own eyes narrowed intently. Mallory's heart tried to plug her throat with its wild beating.

This reaction was purely physical, she told herself
in a panic. She wasn't ready for anything else.
Couldn't be. The last thing she wanted to notice
was the way a lock of his midnight hair clung to
his forehead. Nor did she want to see the squareness
of his jaw, its lines sharpened by that morning's
careful shave.

Helplessly, she looked downward, noting the
other things about him that she didn't want to consider—his shoulders, wide and flat beneath his blue
plaid shirt, darkened here and there by water drop-
lets; the strong column of his throat, the breadth
of his chest, the leanness of his waist. She didn't
want to look at him and feel anything, and yet she
couldn't stop her heart from doing a slow, soft roll
in her chest.

She didn't know how many seconds, or minutes,
she had stared at him, but his eyes had widened in
surprise, then fixed on her as if to see what she
would do. She felt frozen in place, and when she
didn't move, he did, stepping forward with his hand
outstretched. ''Mallory...''

''Mallory,'' Sammi called her from the other
room. She stumbled back as if snatched from the
edge of a precipice. Gasping, she turned away,
grateful to her sister for rescuing her from what
would have been a mistake. She left the bathroom,
glad to be putting distance between them, though
Jack wasn't far behind. She found her sister
standing by the front door, looking down the pock-
marked driveway.

''Mallory, someone's coming,'' she said, as a
Jeep topped the rise and roared over the gravel to

the door. Garnet, still ground-tied in front, tossed her head and shied away, then settled back to eating grass.

The Jeep stopped and a young man stepped out and looked around. His gaze darted around the yard as if taking in everything at once. Mallory was impressed by the quick intelligence in his eyes and the way his face lit up when he saw Garnet. He strolled over to give her a friendly pat on her glossy neck before he came to the front door. Sammi melted back shyly, leaving Mallory and Jack in the opening.

Jack gestured the other man inside. "Morning, T.C. Come in and meet the Earps."

T.C. nodded and stepped into the house. He gave Jack's damp face and jacket a surprised look, but didn't comment as he removed his hat. He nodded to Mallory, who smiled back and murmured a greeting. She noted that he was several inches shorter and much slighter than Jack, but had eyes the identical shade of green and a dimple that emerged at the edge of his mouth. She wondered if he was a relative. She was about to ask when Sammi stepped forward. T.C. straightened and stared at her.

Mallory saw the thunderstruck look in his eyes and turned to look at her sister. Sammi did look exceptionally pretty that morning in an apricot-colored sweater and slacks outfit. Her shiny chestnut hair floated soft and free around her shoulders. She also looked incredibly young and sweet.

"Mallory, Samantha, I'd like you to meet my nephew, T.C. Barrett. T.C., this is Mallory and Samantha Earp. T.C. works for me," Jack said, pride in his voice. "He's one of the best carpenters in this part of the country. He's going to help me work up the estimate."

T.C. gave his uncle a self-conscious smile, then he nodded again to Mallory. "Hello, Miss Earp. I was surprised to hear you'd bought this place. Everybody's talking about it today."

"I hope they're saying good things."

He grinned at his uncle. "They're saying it's good to have Earps back in town."

While Mallory gave Jack a superior look, which he answered with a lift of his eyebrows, T.C. turned his attention to Sammi. She smiled her gentle smile and offered her hand as she looked straight into his eyes. "Hello, T.C., I'm happy to meet you."

T.C. blinked, swallowed hard, clapped his hat over his heart, and took her hand as carefully as if he was capturing an injured baby bird. "I'm happy to meet you, too, Samantha," he said, his voice low. He gazed at her for a long moment, then he smiled at her with such sweetness that Mallory could hear Sammi's breath catch. Color climbed into her cheeks and a light began to glow in her eyes. T.C.'s smile stretched into a grin and they stood like that for several seconds without speaking. The two of them could have been the only ones in the room.

Mallory met Jack's eyes questioningly. He tilted his head as if to say that he didn't know what was going on. Mallory knew, though. It was a look she'd never seen on her sister's face before, but it was unmistakable. She must have been looking at Jack the same way five minutes ago in the bathroom.

"Would you like me to show you around outside, T.C.?" Sammi offered in her quiet way. "My sister says I can have animals here." She looked up at him with her brown eyes shining. "Do you think you could build some pens for me?"

T.C. looked as though he would happily walk over hot coals for her. "I would be glad to," he said. The two of them went outside, leaving Mallory with her jaw sagging.

"What's the matter with you?" Jack demanded.

She turned wide eyes to him. "She's never warmed up to *anyone* so quickly. It usually takes her weeks to get used to new people."

"T.C.'s not just anyone. He's a nice kid. What's the big deal?"

"It's . . . it's not a big deal," she answered defensively, then berated herself for letting him push her into that position once again. "Sammi is . . . special. She's not like other girls her age."

Jack's frown was growing impatient. "Not like other girls. What do you mean? She has a secret life as an international spy? What?"

"No, no." Mallory flapped her hand at him impatiently. "I mean she's always been slower than others her age. She was born when my parents were well into their forties. She was somewhat delayed in her development . . . things never came easily for her . . ." She paused, wondering how much more to say.

"A late bloomer," he supplied, cutting straight to the heart of the matter.

"Well, yes. We've always protected her, and..."

He stared at her. "And you're worried about T.C.? He would never..." His eyes narrowed to suspicious slits. "Wait a minute, you're not worried about that old Earp/Clanton thing, are you?"

She waved that idea away, too. "Of course not. I just don't want to see her hurt."

Jack shook his head. "Hurt?" he asked incredulously. "They just met! Don't you think you're jumping the gun?"

Of course she was, but she couldn't explain her reasons to him, a virtual stranger.

When she didn't respond, he continued, "I noticed last night that you tend to draw wild conclusions. Believe me, T.C.'s the last person you should be worried about." He turned away. "Come on, show me the kitchen."

Chastened, she followed him, pointing out the worst problems and telling him her thoughts about gutting the kitchen and building a more efficient one. He took notes and measurements and made suggestions.

His cool professionalism was in perfect contrast to her own stirring emotions. She was grateful to have a few minutes to catch her breath. It seemed that since he had walked in the door, she had been flung from one emotional peak to another.

It was crazy, but still, she couldn't escape the thought that matters had drastically changed in only a few seconds.

CHAPTER FOUR

MALLORY and Sammi's shop, Passing Time, was located on Allen Street near the Bird Cage Theatre.

When she had first seen the shop, Mallory felt its location must be a good one because of the number of tourists who visited the infamous saloon and bawdy house. Once she had examined the books and seen the stability of the business, she had been convinced to buy it. It had an eclectic mix of merchandise from books about the Old West to antique jewelry and glassware, Apache pottery and natural skin care products produced in an Arizona town famous for its hot springs and mineral baths.

The weekend before, they had moved out of Mallory's apartment in Tucson. The tiny upstairs apartment they were to share until their house was ready had appalled Sammi even more than the place outside of town. There was a living room/kitchen combination, a bathroom and a tiny bedroom barely big enough for their twin beds. Mallory didn't mind because she knew it was only temporary and she attributed Sammi's distress to her need for security. Once they moved into their house and settled into a routine, she was convinced that Sammi would be fine.

During the first days of ownership, she and Sammi were exhausted from the double stress of settling into the apartment and learning the business, but to Mallory's delight, Sammi was catching on quickly. Because their merchandise was bar-coded and they had a computerized cash register, it had been easy for Sammi to learn how to make a cash sale. Mallory still had to help with credit cards, but it wouldn't be long before her sister could be left alone in the shop.

She and Sammi had called their parents, who seemed pleased about their success. Their father had teased Mallory that she was striding into her new life, hauling her somewhat reluctant sister along with her. She had to admit that was true, but she was sure things would work out.

She was especially excited about her house. The home she had shared with Charles, and everything in it, had been done strictly to his taste and she'd had very little say in it.

In her mind, she had decorated the place she was buying with fat, comfortable sofas, billowing white curtains at the windows and jars of fresh potpourri in every room. She couldn't afford all the furnishings yet, but planned to buy a few pieces at a time until it was just right.

Jack was due to drop by anytime with the repair estimate for the house. She hadn't seen him since the previous Saturday, but she had seen plenty of T.C. Mallory sighed inwardly. It was true that T.C. was a perfect gentleman around Sammi, with emphasis on the word "gentle". He treated her with worshipful respect and Sammi was frankly mad about him. Mallory hoped it was only a crush and that T.C. had the good sense not to try to take it further. Now that a few days had passed, she couldn't recall what had alarmed her so much on Saturday. On this beautiful morning, nothing seemed worth worrying about.

She grabbed the broom and went outside to sweep the sidewalk in front of the store and then stood looking up and down the street. Her gaze lingered on the Bird Cage, which had been preserved much as it had been during Tombstone's wildest days. Not only was it interesting from a historical standpoint, but she was sure the customers were titillated by the idea that the prostitutes, of which the Bird Cage had many, had held their assignations with their "johnnies" in the tiny rooms built along the top of the walls. Separated from the patrons below by only a short distance, a low wall and a velvet curtain, the "soiled doves" had practiced the world's oldest profession. Appalling though it was, it had been a common occurrence in the Old West.

Mallory leaned on her broom idly gazing at the imposing building, then looked up the street toward the high school, where classes had been dismissed for the summer and the senior class had graduated. She liked this town, liked the busy but not frantic pace of life. It pleased her to know that although the town was famous for its past, it didn't live in the past but planned for the future.

Her future would be good here—hers and Sammi's. They had options and possibilities that hadn't been available to women in Tombstone's early days.

With her thoughts centered on this, Mallory went back to her sweeping. An idea began forming in her mind. She swept more and more slowly until

she stopped altogether and hurried into the shop.
She hunted up a box full of photo reproductions
that she had found in the shop's existing stock. As
far as she could tell, all of them were of famous
Tombstone shady ladies of the 1880s and 1890s.
Sifting through them, she marveled at the brazen-
ness of their poses and the downright hardness and
homeliness of some of their faces. She concluded
that Tombstone's silver miners must have been truly
anxious for female companionship.

Mallory had marked the photos to half price just
to get them out of her shop. Now she reconsidered.
She was a businesswoman after all, and she knew
that display and advertising were everything. She
picked out the least offensive photos, grabbed an
old-fashioned fringed shawl from the back room,
and loaded her arms with Victorian sachets, bath
bubbles, bath salts and scents from her stock.

She carried everything to the front window, removed the old display of antique glassware, and
spread out the shawl. Then she climbed into the
window and began arranging the photos and scents
in an eye-catching display.

She was just finishing up when a tap on the
window made her glance around. Jack was grinning
at her from the sidewalk.

She raised her voice so she could be heard
through the glass. "Good morning." She backed
out of the window, climbed down to the floor, and
came around to open the door for him.

"Good morning," he responded, stepping inside.
In jeans and a softly faded chambray shirt, he appeared ready for work. He pointed to the photo-

graph in her hand. "You do realize that all these are ladies of the evening, right?"

Mallory glanced at the window where several of the photos were of women in gaudy feathers and fake jewels. "I didn't think they were Sunday school teachers." She pointed to the sachets and bath salts. "I decided to do something different from the displays of Victorian mothers and babies who are usually trotted out to advertise these products."

He tugged on his ear. "Oh, this ought to do it, all right, but somebody might wonder what you're selling here."

Mallory treated him to a superior look. "If they want to know, they'll have to come inside. Did you just drop by to brighten my day, or did you bring the estimate for my house?"

He tapped a folded sheet of paper in his pocket. "I brought the estimate, but I knew you'd be thrilled to see me, too."

Mallory bit the inside of her cheek to keep from laughing. Darn it, why did he have to be so appealing? She didn't want this. No way was she ready for this.

He gestured to the pictures of the "soiled doves". "It's been rumored that this was the profession of Wyatt Earp's third wife."

Ah, this she could deal with. "You mean Josie? How nice for him to get a woman with experience."

Jack threw back his head and laughed. "You never give an inch, do you?"

Although she didn't want to, Mallory found herself experiencing prickles of delight at the deep sound. "I try not to," she admitted with a quirky smile. "And you should learn not to listen to rumors." She tossed the remaining pictures in the box and dusted her hands. "Can I see the estimate now?"

He slipped the paper out and handed it to her. "Yes, ma'am." He folded his arms across his chest and leaned against the doorjamb.

Mallory took it and flipped it open. Carefully, she studied the projected cost of the repairs and renovations. She was pleasantly surprised to see that it was almost exactly what she had budgeted to spend after she'd figured in the addition of another bedroom.

Happiness shone in her face as she looked up at Jack. "This looks fine. In fact, it's great. I can't tell you what it means to have a place of our own."

His eyes met hers. "Everyone needs someplace to belong," he said with quiet seriousness.

Mallory refolded the estimate with a delighted sigh. "Then I guess Tombstone is where we belong. When can you start?"

Slowly, Jack straightened away from the door frame. His eyes tracked the joy in her eyes and the soft flush on her cheeks. His teasing smile softened, making her feel as though melted butter had begun pouring through her veins. "Whenever you say, Mallory. It's up to you."

Why did she suddenly have the feeling that they were no longer talking about the house?

She had to concentrate hard to form an answer. "Soon, then," she said. She stared up at him, noting the slight sheen of the smooth skin on his jaw and smelling the tang of his after-shave, a familiar brand her father often used. Somehow, it didn't trigger thoughts of her sweet, comfortable father, though. It made her recall how long it had been since she'd been close to or held tightly by a virile, sexy man.

The green of his eyes darkened as he looked at her. They touched on several points of her features, then settled on her lips. Mallory couldn't keep herself from treating his to a similar inspection. His mouth was firm, not full like her own. She wondered what it would feel like if the two of them were to touch. Would the contact seal them together in a oneness that would block out the rest of the world?

Would it be as violently explosive as she feared?

When his mouth opened, she almost raised herself on tiptoes, wrapped her arms around his neck, and found out for herself. When he spoke, her attention darted to his knowing eyes.

"Oh, yes," he answered. "We'll start soon."

"Really?" she sighed, settling onto her heels. At this moment, she wouldn't mind starting anything at all that he suggested.

"We're almost finished with our current job."

The practical statement brought her back to earth with a crash. "What?"

"The house," he prompted, but his voice and expression were ripe with amusement.

"Oh!" Heat rushed into her face. "Yes. Oh, yes, of course. The house." She cleared her throat. "That sounds fine."

She crackled the paper between her fingers as if it was some kind of lifeline to reality. What on earth had she been thinking? How could she have forgotten where she was, who she was with, that Sammi would be coming downstairs ready for work any second now?

She cleared her throat again. "Thank you for bringing this estimate over. I've got to get back to my window display." She had meant to sound brisk and businesslike, but her words came out in a breathless rush. She had hoped to prompt him on his way, but instead, he stood where he was, considering her.

"Mallory, if you're going to live in this town, you need to know more about its history."

She drew back. "I know a great deal about its history."

"But have you heard it from the Clanton side?"

"I've never cared for fairy tales."

That got his eyes to glowing. "Oh, really?"

What was the matter with her? She'd never been this reckless before, but she crossed her arms over her chest. "Yes, really."

"Don't be a coward. How about a few lessons?" He glanced at her mouth. "In history, I mean."

"I know everything I need to know, at least for now. Thank you anyway."

"Meaning you're afraid of learning the truth. Customers will be asking you questions about this town. You'd better know the answers."

"I can simply refer them to you since you know everything."

He held up his hand. "Don't you know knowledge is power?"

"You think I want power over my customers?" she asked in a flat voice.

"Sure you do. Power to keep them in your shop long enough to buy something. People spend more money in a friendly atmosphere than an unfriendly one."

"I'll try to remember to only be unfriendly with you."

"Too late for that. I'll be working on your house, remember?"

Mallory gave him a sour look. "That can be changed."

Jack tapped the paper in her hand. "No, it can't."

He truly had an answer for everything. Still, she couldn't, wouldn't give up. She felt compelled to make him understand who was the boss. "You're right," she admitted. "I wouldn't have hired you if I hadn't thought you would do a good job."

He gave her a look that said he was too much of a gentleman to point out that she'd had very little choice in the matter.

"However," she went on, "I fully intend to be involved in the work on my house."

His brows drew together. "Define 'involved'."

"I'll be there to watch every phase of the repairs to make sure I'm getting what I'm paying for."

Jack looked pained. "Just don't get in the way."

"It's my house."

"It's my crew... and my job."

"Well, yes, of course, but—" The phone rang, interrupting her. "Excuse me," she said, turning toward the front counter. "I'll just be a moment."

She picked up the receiver and said, "Passing Time. This is Mallory speaking. May I help you?" It gave her such a thrilling jolt to say those words that she treated Jack to an unexpectedly friendly grin. He smiled back and winked at her.

"Mallory? Heavens, you sound just like a shop girl."

Her face went blank with surprise and her stomach flopped over like a grounded fish. "Charles?"

"Hello, darling. I'm just calling to see how you're doing with your little business venture."

Mallory's fingers wrapped around the receiver. "Why would you care?"

After a moment's hurt silence, he said, "Mallory, dear, I've always cared about you and about what you're doing."

"As long as it was what you wanted me to do." Her reply had come out more sharply than she expected. Across the room, Jack turned to look at her. Anyone else would have removed themselves to a polite distance out of earshot. Jack, of course, moved closer.

"That's not true," he soothed. "You know I've always wanted you to grow and develop as a person."

Mallory rolled her eyes.

"And I want to make sure you're happy and that your business is going well. After all, I earned the money that you're using to buy it."

A wave of red washed before her eyes. "No, Charles. *I* earned the money. I did the research for both of your books. I typed the manuscript. In fact,

I wrote most of the first draft. I *earned* my divorce settlement and don't you ever think differently."

"Of course, dear. I wasn't trying to belittle your contribution."

In her mind's eye, Mallory could see his patrician features taking on a pained look. She was sure he thought it made him appear as if he was being empathetic, but in truth, he looked as if he was suffering from indigestion. "Yes, Charles, you were and we both know it. Now, why did you call?"

He gave an aggrieved sigh. "Merely to wish you and little Sammi all the best. She's doing well, I trust."

"Not that you really care, but yes, she's fine, thank you." Mallory's face was burning, and with each passing second, she was aware of Jack Clanton, who restlessly wandered the room, unashamedly listening to every word.

"I care about your little sister, but you know it wouldn't have worked out to have her living with us. We both needed space, and—"

"Now you have all the space you could possibly want, don't you, Charles? Listen, why don't I simply take this call in the spirit in which it was intended, if, that is, you intended kindness or are even capable of kind feelings."

"Really, Mallory, there's no need for you to be so vulgar—"

"Goodbye, Charles. My obligation to you is at an end, our marriage is at an end, and so is this conversation." She set the receiver carefully on the hook and stood staring at it for several seconds, breathing deeply and trying to control her anger and asking herself for the zillionth time how she'd ever imagined herself in love with that jerk. Even more incomprehensible, how had she stayed married to him for six years?

"Problems?" Jack asked, coming to stand on the opposite side of the counter.

Distracted, she glanced up and saw that his jaw was set and a line of white had appeared around his tight mouth.

He looked furious. Mallory blinked and drew back. He couldn't be angry on her behalf, could he?

"No," she denied automatically, because she was too surprised by his reaction to think of anything to say. "It's... I'm fine."

Jack studied her for a moment as if he wanted to push her to give him a more honest answer. The proud tilt of her head told him she wouldn't be pushed. Finally, the expression on his face eased, shifting into his usual easygoing smile. "I'll be on my way, then." He turned away, then glanced back. "Don't forget my offer to be your tour guide."

Glad that he hadn't pushed her, she smirked at him. "What a kind offer. I'll consider it."

"You do that," he said in a voice as smooth as French silk. "Let me know when you're ready."

Mallory stared at him while a feeling of anticipation shimmered through her. She was beginning to learn that it was far more likely that *he* would tell *her* when she was ready.

"Mallory, we need to have a little talk." Jack spoke abruptly from the doorway.

Mallory jumped and nearly tumbled off the ladder where she was perching. As Jack had decreed, she'd been careful to stay out of the way while she offered advice to Fred and Jim on the proper laying of her bathroom tile. Fred had repaired the leaking pipes that had sapped the water pressure and replaced the shower head so it would no longer squirt people in the face.

In only two weeks' time, vast improvements could be seen in her house. The roof had been replaced and the ceiling repaired. Even the new bedroom and bathroom addition was taking shape with the concrete floor poured and the foundation laid for the adobe walls. Stacks of adobe blocks were neatly lined up, ready to be laid.

Mallory loved every minute of the construction. Whenever she felt she could leave Sammi alone in the shop, she hurried to the house to be involved in the work.

She liked being around Fred and Jim, who were hardworking and thorough. The three of them had been having a fascinating discussion about the local construction business and Jack's part in it.

From the Jackman brothers, she had learned how very wrong she had been about Jack and his business success. After listening to them for a while, she realized that poverty wasn't the reason he drove a six-year-old truck and lived in a small apartment.

He was generous to his employees, but he didn't spend much money on himself because every spare cent went back into his business or to buy real estate. He valued financial security for himself and his employees more than he desired frills. The only thing he'd ever really wanted was the house his grandfather had built and his mother had been forced to sell when the family needed money. It made Mallory squirm to realize she was the reason he'd been denied that one wish. However, she didn't really feel guilty because she loved the house so much.

Jack had been in Phoenix on business for a couple of days, which had suited her just fine. When she didn't see him, it was easy for her to forget what a formidable impact he had on her.

Seeing him standing in the doorway, though, with the sleeves of his soft chamois shirt rolled up and his cowboy hat pushed to the back of his head, she remembered all too well. The trick was to not let it affect her.

She blinked innocently at the glowering man and blessed him with her sunniest smile. "Yes, Jack, what can I do for you?"

He stepped around a box of tile grout and over a pile of the six-inch Mexican-made squares that Fred and Jim had stacked nearby. He came to stand directly in front of her.

Mallory immediately decided she didn't like the look in his eyes. The pale green seemed to have undergone a transformation that reminded her of approaching thunderclouds.

"For one thing, you can get out of here and let these two men do their jobs."

Mallory straightened and lifted her chin at him. "They are doing their jobs. I'm only watching."

"And offering suggestions and telling them what to do and distracting them."

Mallory touched her hand to her throat. "Distracting them? Me?"

At that moment, Jim and Fred exchanged a look, lumbered to their feet and said, "Boss, we'll take a little break now. It's gettin' mighty hot in here."

From the look on Jack's face, she thought it was probably going to get a great deal hotter.

Jim and Fred squeezed out of the room, leaving her alone with Jack and all too aware of how much of the room he seemed to fill. Funny, it hadn't seemed so full even with both the Jackman brothers in there.

Jack placed his hands at his waist and rocked back on his boot heels. "I hear you've been spending quite a bit of time here while I've been gone."

"It's my house." Mallory knew she should stand up and face him toe-to-toe, but she feared that a change in her position would signal that he made her feel defensive or uncomfortable.

"That can still be remedied," he countered, but when she ignored his veiled offer to buy her out, he went on. "I know it's your house, but, as I told you before, this is my job."

"And you think I'm interfering?"

"I know you are. T.C. tells me you're here more than you're at your shop."

"And he should know, since he's at the shop more than he's here," she said, then bit her tongue. She was trying to keep a watch on the situation with T.C. and Sammi without being ridiculously obsessive.

Jack's eyes sharpened. "Still worried about my nephew and your sister?"

"I'm simply watching out for her. She's only eighteen."

"Which means she's an adult in everyone's eyes but yours," he pointed out. When she started to protest, he held up his hand. "Save it. I didn't come to talk about that. I'm here to remind you that you hired me and my crew to do this job, right?"

Although she felt angry heat washing into her face, she answered in a level tone. "That's right."

"Then you've got to stay away and let us do the job."

"I'm not a novice at this, you know."

Jack cocked his head and looked at her skeptically. "Oh, really?"

"Yes. My father owned a hardware store in Illinois before he retired. I helped him out from the time I could barely see over the counter."

"And you think that qualifies you to give advice on laying tile and plastering walls?"

That brought her to her feet. "Absolutely. It's my house."

He shook his head. "Mallory, it doesn't work that way. You hired us to do the job. Stay out of the way and let us do it. We're professionals. You don't know what you're doing."

Mallory's lips drew together and two spots of color rode high on her cheeks. She knew he was frustrated with her, but in it she could see shadows from her marriage with Charles. In his tone, she heard echoes of Charles's disdainful voice whenever she tried anything new. "Maybe I don't. After all, I hired you, Mr. Clanton."

Jack stuck his chin forward until it almost touched hers. "And maybe you're thinking you can get out of our agreement, hmm, Miss Earp? That's not going to happen. Remember that handshake? Like I told you, around here that's binding. And you're sticking to it."

She wanted to tell him exactly what he could do with his agreement, but she couldn't. It would be devastating to see her house go unfinished. "I wouldn't dream of breaking our agreement, Mr. Clanton. I always stick to my word." She smiled, unable to resist a little dig. "You could even say it's a family trait."

That kindled a fire of competition in his eyes. He stepped back and looked at her. "Meaning the Earp family?"

"Meaning the Earp family."

Jack looked at her with narrow-eyed intent. He lifted his hand and rested his strong chin on the knuckle of his first finger. "Mallory, I believe you're challenging me to set you and your facts straight."

She blinked at him, but held her own. This had gone from being a business disagreement to being a refighting of the old feud. She had trouble keeping up with him. She didn't even attempt to stay ahead of him, but darn it, she wasn't going to look foolish, either.

"My facts are just fine, thank you. I think it's your facts that need help."

His eyes darkened. "Are you calling me out?"

"That's right. To a showdown."

"You mean a walkdown."

She crossed her arms and gave him a defiant look even though she knew he was right. The famous Western cliché where two men met in the middle of the street ready to shoot it out while frightened townspeople ran for cover was called a walkdown because of the slow manner in which the opponents approached each other.

With his tough features shaded by his cowboy hat, his muscles lovingly hugged by his snug shirt, and his big hands resting on his hips, he could easily have passed for a gunslinger. With the devil-may-care look in his eyes and a lock of hair feathered down over his forehead, he could even more easily pass for a lady-killer.

Mallory felt tension coil inside her and an effervescence surge upward. It took her several seconds to realize it was excitement. Disconcerted, she temporarily lost her train of thought, which gave Jack the advantage.

"I think it's time we settled this," he went on.

"Name the time and the place."

"Your shop closes at five, right?"

She nodded.

"Then 5:05 in front of the Bird Cage."

"I have to close out my cash drawer and make my bank deposit," she answered.

"Then we'll make it six o'clock." He turned away, then glanced back. "Once we set your facts straight, I'll buy you dinner. Never let it be said I'm a gloating winner."

"Never let it be said I'm a loser—of any kind."
Her voice was flippant, but an adventurous spirit
was running through her, making her reckless. "I'll
meet you there."

Jack gave her a casual two-fingered salute that
she was coming to recognize as a local custom and
headed out the door. Once he was out of sight,
Mallory pressed her hands to her stomach and took
a deep breath. She was crazy to meet him as he
demanded, but she wouldn't back down. She was
looking forward to six o'clock.

CHAPTER FIVE

MALLORY saw Jack as soon as she called goodbye to her sister, stepped into the warm spring evening, and closed the door behind her. Dressed in black jeans and a pale green shirt, he was leaning against a wooden signpost planted in the ground before the Bird Cage Theatre. Above his head was a sign stating this was the spot where Tombstone Marshal Fred White had been killed by "Curly Bill" Brocius.

Mallory's lips quirked as soon as she saw where he was standing. It was obvious that he intended to carry this modern-day version of the Earp/Clanton feud as far as he could. She intended to make sure he didn't have it all his own way.

She stepped to the edge of the boardwalk, looked both ways up and down the narrow street that could barely accommodate the passing of two cars, and sauntered over to Jack. She had changed clothes, debating over various outfits until she had told herself not to be silly. This wasn't a date. She had finally settled on the patterned broomstick skirt and gold sweater she'd worn the night they met, reasoning it was comfortable and not too dressy. She had time only to freshen her makeup and brush her long hair back from her face. Loose and free, it hung to her waist.

Jack's back came away from the signpost when he saw her. He stood with his thumbs hooked in his back pockets and his palms turned outward, one of those relaxed poses that were so natural to him even when his eyes were sharply interested as they were now.

He met her eyes and Mallory couldn't mistake the approval there. He thought she was attractive, and in spite of the conflicts between them and her own doubts, she found that gratifying and exciting.

As she stepped up beside him, he pulled his hands from his pockets and jerked his thumb toward the sign. "This looks like as good a place as any to start. After all, much of the trouble between the Earps and the Clantons began when Fred White died."

Mentally, she rubbed her hands together. Maybe he didn't have all his facts after all. "The trouble started when the Clantons, the McLowerys and their 'cowboy' friends began rustling cattle along the Mexican border and stole six mules from the army."

Jack reached over, took her arm, and pulled her close to him. He gave her a look of mock admiration. "Miss Earp, I think you might know a little bit more about this than I suspected."

She answered him with a demure flutter of her lashes and a droll smile. "Why, Mr. Clanton, the truth is, I know a *great deal* more about this, and a lot of other things, than you suspected."

"We'll see." He started down the boardwalk and she strolled along, too. Their boot heels rang hollowly on the wooden slats. "The shooting was accidental, you know. Curly Bill and his buddies were just having a little friendly target practice at the moon when Marshal White tried to take Bill's pistol."

"How very foolish of Marshal White."

Jack tucked her slim hand into the crook of his elbow and gave her a severe look, but laughter brimmed in his eyes. "Sarcasm is really unattractive on you."

Her own laughter bubbled up. "I'll try to control it."

"Good. Now, where were we?"

"You were giving me your highly fabricated and entertaining version of the events leading up to Marshal White's death."

"Fabricated?"

"Sorry. It just slipped out."

"Pay attention. Your ancestor, Wyatt, a deputy sheriff of Pima County, had been in a local saloon, where he spent a great deal of his time—"

"Like most men of the West," she added innocently. "After all, as my ancestor Wyatt said, there were no Young Men's Christian Associations in the Wild West. Saloons were their social clubs."

Jack considered her for a few seconds. "Point taken. However, we're not going to get through this if you keep interrupting."

"Excuse me," she said humbly.

"When Marshal White saw Wyatt coming to help, he grabbed Curly Bill's pistol. It went off and shot Marshal White. Wyatt 'buffaloed' Curly Bill by cracking him on the head with the handle of a pistol he had borrowed from a bystander. White lived long enough to absolve Curly Bill of blame, but Bill was mad at Wyatt for pistol-whipping him and embarrassing him in front of the town. That was the second incident between the Earps and the group that was known as the 'cowboys'.''

''The term 'cowboy' was a derogatory one at that time. They were called that because they rustled cows,'' Mallory added in a pedantic tone. Jack lifted an eyebrow at her and she grinned as she said, ''What happened next?''

''Not long after that, Wyatt resigned as deputy sheriff because two friends of his were running against each other for sheriff and he didn't want to take sides.''

''Oh, is that the election in which your ancestor, Ike Clanton, stuffed the ballot box in the San Simon Valley so that the man he supported would win?''

Jack stopped to consider that one, looking up into the dusky sky as if pulling the answer from outer space. After a moment, he said, ''Yeah, I guess it was. So?''

''So, what do you think of that?''

Jack arranged his face into an expression of comical modesty and said, ''We Clantons have always been a very civic-minded bunch of folks.''

Exasperated, Mallory pointed her finger at him. ''There were one hundred fraudulent ballots in the box.''

Jack stopped on the corner across from the Crystal Palace and rubbed his chin thoughtfully. ''Maybe one hundred was as high as old Ike could count. He wasn't the brightest member of the family.''

Mallory rolled her eyes at him and said, "No kidding." She tugged on his arm. "Let's keep going."

They walked on, nodding to people as they passed, discussing and arguing over the roles each of their respective ancestors had in the series of confrontations that had taken place throughout 1881. Jack argued that while the Clantons and the McLowerys may have occasionally skipped along on the wrong side of the law, they weren't much worse than many people who lived and worked in the area at that time. In its earliest days, Tombstone had been part of Pima County, but was too far away from Tucson for law enforcement to be effective. Many locals had simply taken advantage of the situation.

Mallory argued back that they were still guilty of breaking the law. She even convinced Jack to admit that Virgil Earp had been an excellent town marshal for Tombstone, maintaining law and order and enforcing local ordinances throughout his term.

They both admitted that their respective ancestors had been opportunists—the Earps as investors in gambling operations and speculators in mines, and the Clantons as "liberators" of cattle whose ownership they considered to be questionable.

As they walked and talked, Mallory occasionally thought of the scholarly discussions she'd once tried to have with Charles on matters of history.

As if he could read her thoughts, Jack gave her a shrewd look and said, "Where did you learn so much about the history of this area? In college?"

Her lips twisted ruefully. "I guess you could say that. My ex-husband is a professor of history. I was his research assistant."

"That was him on the phone the other day."

"That's right." She grimaced. Charles had called twice more since that day. Each time, he had been full of unctuous concern. He had even offered to give her money if her "little shop" ran into financial troubles. Mallory was mystified about the reason for these calls. She certainly hadn't encouraged them.

Jack frowned and shook his head. "I've studied in this field, too, and I don't recall hearing of a professor named Earp..."

"That's *my* name, remember? I took it back when my divorce was final. His name is Garrison."

Jack stopped so suddenly his upper body bent forward, then back. His head snapped around and he said, "Not *Charles* Garrison."

"I see you've heard of him."

"I took a class from him once. Whatever made you marry that pompous windbag?"

Mallory rubbed the toe of one boot against the heel of the other and looked off into the distance, wishing that she'd never brought it up. She couldn't imagine what had possessed her except that for the first time since they'd met, she'd felt relaxed with Jack. She didn't want to talk about her marriage. Even though a year had passed, she still felt foolish, and there were some parts of the wound Charles had left that were still raw.

"Mallory," Jack prompted. His voice had gone from a light, teasing tone to the no-nonsense command she'd heard so often before.

"That's personal, Jack, and—"

"You brought it up," he broke in, echoing her own thoughts.

She stared at him for a few seconds. Oh, well. She might as well tell him. He would find out eventually simply because he was so persistent.

"Youthful idiocy," she sighed. "Hero worship. I don't know."

She could tell that Jack wasn't satisfied with that answer, but he only said, "He must be twelve years older than you are."

"More like fifteen." Mallory reached up with both hands and tossed her hair back over her shoulders, then looked into Jack's eyes. He wanted to ask more. She could see it. She could feel it in the force of his powerful will as he met her gaze. He wanted to ask about her life with Charles, but she didn't want to tell him.

The reluctance must have been obvious, because Jack studied her for a few more seconds, then said, "Come on. Our tour isn't finished."

She gave him a grateful look as he continued.

"The events that happened here weren't the end of it," Jack was saying, and Mallory looked up to see that they had stopped before the O.K. Corral. "In fact, the famous gunfight didn't even happen in the corral, but in a small lot next to it. If they'd all taken time to cool off, nothing would have happened."

She nodded and looked up at the tall wooden gates of the corral. "What a sad waste."

Jack snorted. "Yeah, but the Clantons got the worst of it."

"I know. Billy Clanton was killed and he was only nineteen—sadly misguided into a life of crime and he died because of it."

Jack startled her by grasping her elbow and sliding his hand down her arm. Grabbing her other hand, he pulled her around to face him. His eyes were full of amusement when he said, "Now there you go, starting up the old argument all over again."

"You didn't think I was going to actually admit that my forebears might have been wrong, did you?"

"Possibly that would have been too much to expect."

Mallory relaxed into a smile. Her hands were warm in his. She felt oddly safe and secure. "Does this mean neither of us won the argument?"

"I'd call it a draw," he admitted.

She pursed her lips consideringly and gave him a sly look from beneath her lashes. "So you won't be buying me dinner?"

His gaze was focused on her lips. "Well, what do you know? I guess I did win and I have to pay off."

Mallory smiled at him, letting the pleasure run through her. She didn't know where her sudden flirtatiousness had come from—a long-buried tendency toward recklessness, perhaps—or why she'd been so frightened of this feeling of attraction. He was tough and pushy, but he wasn't going to force anything on her. "So let's go," she said.

Jack took her hand and led her over one block to the Bella Union Restaurant, where he bought her a steak and they shared a bottle of wine. They continued their discussion but they didn't stick to that one topic. Before long, he brought the subject around to old legends and hidden treasures and she found herself talking once again about Lying Jude Bluestone's stolen money and her belief that it was still somewhere in the Chiricahua Mountains.

The minute she broached the subject, Jack's eyes began to glow with interest. He poured more red wine into her glass and said, "Why do you think it's still there? That all happened in 1895. Besides, most people believe the deputy sheriff found it and got rich on it."

Mallory took a sip of the wine and settled back into her chair. In spite of its rather elegant name, the Bella Union was homey, not fancy, and the food had been good. She glanced around at the other diners and wondered how many of them were locals as she and Jack were and how many were visitors. Most people who came to Tombstone were interested in the history of the feud between her and Jack's famous relatives. Few of them realized that the entire area was rich in history.

Jack knew, though, and she was enjoying talking it over with him. She was surprised at how relaxed and at ease she felt. "I've done more research on it than just about anybody else. It's true that George Early, the deputy sheriff, went after Jude and came back empty-handed, and then seemed to be flush with money soon afterward. However, he explained all that when he said he'd come into a recent inheritance.''

Jack had removed his hat and placed it on an empty chair so that she had a full view of his face. A troubled frown creased his forehead. ''Not many people believed that story.''

''They didn't bother to look into the family records back in Missouri where George had come from. Although he was an orphan, he had a great-aunt in St. Joseph who remembered him in her will.''

''People believe what they want to believe, Mallory,'' he said in a dry tone. ''George had a letter from the lawyer, which he showed around town, but people didn't believe him.''

Mallory sat forward. ''You know the whole story, then?''

''Some of it,'' he hedged. ''You didn't finish what you were saying.'' He poured more wine into her glass. ''Why do you think Jude's stolen treasure is still in the mountains?''

Mallory picked up the glass and sipped the liquid. It was beginning to make her feel just a bit light-headed. The sensation wasn't unpleasant. She smiled at Jack and leaned farther across the table to say in a conspiratorial whisper, ''I've got George Early's journal.''

The wine bottle slipped from Jack's fingers and thumped to the tabletop. He righted it quickly without looking at it. His eyes were fixed on her. ''His journal? George Early's journal?''

She nodded. "That's right."

"Where...? How...?"

Mallory giggled, then covered her mouth. She *had* drunk too much wine. She wasn't a giggling sort of woman.

Jack was staring at her transfixed. Really, he was turning out to be a wonderful audience.

"In his exalted position as an Arizona history authority, Charles is often asked to authenticate documents that turn up unexpectedly. The journal was in a box of papers that came from the estate of a lady in Graham County, who passed away when she was one hundred and three years old. She had received the things from her father, who had been sheriff when George set out after Jude Bluestone."

Jack went very still. He was staring at her, through her, with an expression she couldn't quite read. It was a combination of amazement and hope. "Well, I'll be darned. That's where it was."

Mallory tilted her head and regarded him curiously. While it was gratifying to have an interested audience, she thought he seemed particularly intrigued by the news. "You mean the journal?"

He didn't answer her question, didn't even seem to hear it. He remained motionless for several seconds as if all his strength was concentrated on what was going on in his mind. His hands were still clasped around the wine bottle, the knuckles turning white.

After a while, his eyes cleared and focused on her. "So how did you end up with it?"

Taken aback by that moment of intensity, Mallory took a few seconds to gather her thoughts. "Charles couldn't verify its authenticity. In fact, he said it was a fake because the dates mentioned in it didn't match up with the times George was known to be looking for Jude." She shrugged as she sat back. "So, since the lady had no heirs and no one seemed to want the thing, I got it."

"So why do you think it's genuine?"

Mallory gave him a self-deprecating smile. This was the tricky part, where she tended to lose credibility. Oh, well, at least Jack wasn't a scoffer as Charles had been. Jack might accept her explanation. Still, she couldn't help lifting her chin and daring him to laugh at her. "I have a feeling."

His eyes widened. "You have a feeling?"

"Don't ask me to explain." She waved her hand at him as if to blow off his objections, should he have any. "I'm convinced it's genuine. So much so that I plan to go into the mountains and look for the treasure myself as soon as I can leave Sammi alone in the shop."

Jack drew back and gave her a skeptical look. "You'd do this on the basis of a *feeling*?"

"That's right."

"Taking an awful lot on faith, aren't you? You don't seem like an impulsive woman."

"Maybe not, but you know yourself that I'm a lucky one. Remember when I beat you at poker?"

Jack shook his head and signaled the waitress for coffee. "Luck at cards and luck at finding bank robbery money that's been lost for more than one hundred years are two very different things. There's no guarantee that you'll get lucky."

Mallory lifted her hands, palm up. "There's no guarantee I won't."

"Do you know your way around the Chiricahuas?"

"No, not really," she admitted, though she hated to. This was the part of her plan that wasn't very well thought out. "I intend to hire a guide."

Jack's wide mouth split in a grin. "Are you sure you want to do that? The more people who know, the more who'll follow you into the mountains and dog your every step until you find the money."

"You think they'll conk me on the head and take it away?"

"It's been known to happen. Do you have a map?"

"The journal has details telling which way Jude went into the mountains, how George followed him, although the exact location is vague..."

"But no big black X saying 'dig here'?"

Mallory pushed her coffee away, untouched, shoved the sleeves of her sweater up to her elbows, and drummed her fingers on the tabletop. She was still feeling a bit light-headed, but her mind was clear enough to understand what he was saying. At this moment, he sounded very much like Charles.

"I don't have the whole thing thought out yet. I'm not sure what I'll do after I get as far as George's journal can take me."

"Honey, that much is obvious."

"You think I can't do it?"

Alerted by her aggressive tone, Jack held up his hand. "I didn't say that, but you've got to have a guide who will—"

"Hello, Jack, Miss Earp," a man's voice greeted them. They'd been so engrossed in their discussion, they hadn't noticed his approach. Now Mallory recognized Dan Wilkers, the other man who'd been at the poker game the night she met Jack. With him was a woman whom he introduced as his wife, Susan.

Jack stood up immediately, moved his chair closer to hers, set his hat on a nearby empty table, and hitched up two more chairs. The evening dinner crowd was thinning out, so they pretty much had the place to themselves. Jack invited the other couple to join them for coffee and the subject of Lying Jude's treasure was forgotten.

It was just as well, Mallory decided. She'd said enough about it, and while she had no reason to distrust Jack, she knew her plan wasn't foolproof and she didn't want to invite scorn. Her heart ached to think that that was one of the saddest legacies of her marriage. Even after all this time, she avoided even the possibility that someone she cared about would mock her ideas and opinions.

Surprised by that thought and acknowledging that she did care about him, she watched Jack and listened as he talked to his friends about local happenings. He made a point of drawing her into the conversation and of discussing things of interest to everyone at the table. At no time was there any doubt that he was the host. He had a way of assuming command that was both intriguing and compelling.

She learned that Dan was something of an expert on local history with a special interest in mysteries and disappearances. However, Jack didn't mention Lying Jude, and neither did she. Mallory couldn't help comparing Jack to Charles because her ex-husband was the last man with whom she'd spent an evening out. It hadn't been like this, though. Jack was a fascinating companion. He had held up his end of their debate over their families without resorting to sarcasm or scorn. It gave her an unusually giddy feeling of relief to know she had held her own in their discussion and that her opinion had value. Jack might not agree with her, but he listened.

They parted from Dan and Susan outside the restaurant. Mallory turned toward her shop and the tiny apartment over it, but Jack took her hand and drew her back.

"Come with me. I want to show you something."

"What?"

His grin flashed in the dim light. "You'll see."

Her eyes narrowed suspiciously. "Where is it?"

He tugged her down the boardwalk and she had to scramble to keep up. "Wait and see."

"Are you doing a cryptic, Gary Cooper routine?"

They had reached his truck. Jack pulled the door open and helped her inside. "Don't knock Coop. He was a real cowboy, and besides, one Hollywood starlet said that before his marriage, he was the best lover she ever had."

He slammed the door on Mallory's sputtering protest and trotted around to his own side. When he climbed in and started the engine, Mallory gave him a dark look. She was at a loss for a reply. Trust him to twist her words and change the atmosphere between them to one she didn't welcome—or at least one she told herself she didn't welcome.

Mallory managed to keep her curiosity under control until they pulled into Benson and stopped at a home on the edge of town. In the glow of a bright yard light, she could see that it was a rambling brick structure. Soft lamps glowed invitingly in the windows. Behind the house was a barn and a corral.

When Jack took her hand and helped her out of the truck, Mallory glanced around. "Where are we?"

"My sister's place. Come in and meet her."

Mallory hesitated, not sure she was ready to meet Jack's family. After all, it wasn't as if they'd been on a real date, and they certainly weren't romantically interested in each other. Before she could say anything, though, Jack took her arm and urged her toward the door.

"Don't worry. You'll like her. You've already met the worst member of the family."

"That would be you, I assume?"

"That would be me." He opened the front door and invited her inside, then called out to see if anyone was home.

Within seconds, a trim blonde with a sunny smile came hurrying from the kitchen. Jack introduced his sister, Carolyn Barrett.

With a quick handshake and a warm smile, Carolyn made her feel welcome. "This is great," she said, leading the way back to the kitchen. "We've already met your sister this evening."

"You have?"

"T.C. brought her out, probably for the same reason you're here. Go on out to the corral. I'll join you in a few minutes. I've got a cake in the oven for the church bake sale tomorrow." Briskly, she whipped the oven door open while Jack strode to the back door, taking Mallory with him.

Mallory shook her head in confusion as they stepped onto the porch. "*Why* am I here?"

"Gary, Carolyn's husband, and I are partners in a horse-raising operation. One of the mares foaled today." He indicated the corral and barn and they headed that way.

"Foaled? You mean...a baby horse?"

Jack chuckled. "That's right, city girl. Come and see our new colt."

In a stall fragrant with the scent of new hay, a palomino mare hovered protectively over a knobby-kneed colt who stood shakily as he began to nurse.

Mallory knelt in the hay and gingerly touched his velvety coat. "Oh, he's beautiful," Mallory breathed, drawing her hand away. He turned his head and regarded her solemnly through eyes of melting brown. "I'll bet Sammi went crazy over him."

"She did," Carolyn said, bustling up behind them. She gave her brother a quick grin. "Believe it or not, Gary went into town to buy some cigars.

He's as excited about this as he was when T.C. and Rhonda were born.''

Jack grinned and looked proudly at the newborn. "He has a right to be proud. Ruby's first two foals were stillborn." Mallory was sure that if he'd been wearing suspenders, Jack would have tucked his thumbs into them and puffed out his chest.

The two women exchanged smiles and she realized that she could easily come to like Jack's sister.

Carolyn stayed and chatted a few minutes, then went back to the house, leaving Jack and Mallory alone in the quiet barn.

Mallory leaned her arms on the top rail of the stall. "I like your sister, Jack." She threw him a teasing glance. "She isn't much like you."

He cocked his head. "You mean she's not an irritating pain in the behind?"

"That's right."

When Jack laughed, Mallory felt gooseflesh prickle up her arms and something settled inside her as if a warm hand had cupped itself around her heart.

It would be very easy for her to fall in love with this man.

CHAPTER SIX

JACK's laughter died away, leaving Mallory shaken by her disturbing thought. She lifted a trembling hand to smooth her hair away from her face as she tried to come to terms with it. She couldn't be falling in love with him. She'd thought herself in love before and it had been a disaster. It wasn't love she felt for Jack, but admiration.

To prove it to herself, she focused on the things she liked about him. "You're an unusual man, Jack Clanton. You own your own business where you employ your niece and nephew. You raise horses with your brother-in-law. Jim and Fred tell me you own real estate all over Arizona. It sounds like you believe in diversity."

"I believe in staying out of debt," he said dryly. He was quiet for a minute, then he went on, "Mallory, my family wasn't like yours."

"What do you mean?"

"There was no family business to support us. My dad abandoned us when Carolyn was twelve and I was ten, then our mother died six years later. Carolyn was married to Gary by then and I moved in with them. We were like three kids raising ourselves."

She wanted to tell him he'd done a good job, but couldn't force the words past the lump of compassion that had swelled up in her throat. She

96

thought of the warmth and security of the home where she'd grown up with two parents who had loved, provided for and protected her.

Jack was gazing into the stall as he spoke. "Even before Dad left, he couldn't hold a job for very long. We were so poor growing up that the only thing we had in any amount was our heritage."

"That's why your family and its history are so important to you."

"Yeah."

"That's why you wanted my house."

"Part of the reason."

"Jack?"

"Yes?"

"Did he ever come back?"

"My dad?" He turned his head and stared off as if deep in thought. For a minute, she thought he wasn't going to answer her. "No, but he called whenever he needed money. He was killed about ten years ago, walking along a dark road somewhere in Kentucky. Carolyn and I paid for him to be buried there."

She nodded, thinking of what it must have been like to be abandoned. She was glad he had told her. It made her admiration for him and his accomplishments waver right on the border, almost tumbling over into love.

As they drove back to Tombstone, Mallory reflected on what he'd told her and wondered why he'd done it. She knew she wasn't a coward, but she wasn't sure she was prepared for the answer if she asked him directly.

Back in town, Jack stopped the truck at the end of Allen Street and they walked up to her shop. Mallory dug in the pocket of her skirt for her key.

At her door, he plucked the key from her hand, inserted it in the lock, and opened the door for her. When she turned to take back her key and thank him, she found that he was standing much too close. His broad shoulders blocked out the light from the street lamps.

She looked up, her brown eyes suddenly unsure, her heart seeming to slow its beat, then speed up.

Jack murmured her name, and then his lips were on hers. Mallory sighed into his mouth as the firm touch of his lips sent warmth, and then heat, spiraling through her. His hands slipped up her arms and then over her shoulders to cup her face in a way that made her bones melt. Her own hands rested unsteadily at his waist, then scooted over the hard muscles that banded his back.

At this signal of her acceptance, Jack made a deep, growling sound in his throat and pulled her hard into his embrace. His lips touched her eyes, her cheeks, then came back to ravage her mouth.

His taste went through her in jolts of sensation that were both frightening and wildly arousing. His mouth was firm, warm and commanding. She couldn't get her breath, and then forgot that she needed to breathe.

Why hadn't she expected this? The thought flashed through her mind as her hands dug into his hard muscles, kneading against the rich fabric of his shirt, wishing it was his skin. Why hadn't she expected that a man who did everything with such strength and power would kiss like this?

He was frightening and fulfilling, powerful, potent. Her mind ran out of descriptive words as he drew her even closer, bruising her, crushing her close, making her ache for him.

The swiftness of his passion caused a shaft of fear to spurt through her. Where had his gentleness gone? she wondered hazily. Where was his easygoing teasing now?

She had read him all wrong.

Mallory pulled back. "Jack, don't. I—"

"You what?" he asked in a low tone, lifting his head. His eyes glittered and his breath was ragged, coming in short bursts that puffed against her cheek.

The warmth of it was so inviting, she turned away. "I'm not—"

"Yes, you are," he said, interrupting her with another kiss. "You can't deny what you feel."

How could she deny it when he kissed her again and she lifted her hands to entwine in the thickness of his black hair? How could she tell him no when she wanted him to never stop giving her this heady rush of sensation? He made her feel as if she was the most desirable woman on earth.

"Come home with me, Mallory." His voice was raw, full of the same need she was feeling. "Come with me. Sammi can stay alone for one night."

"No...no. I ca-can't," she stammered, finally gathering the strength to draw away from him. She lifted shaky hands to push back her hair and brush her swollen, tender lips. Her eyes were slumberous and yet edged with shock.

She hadn't been thinking, only feeling. Jack aroused emotions in her she'd never known, not even with Charles. If she'd made such a horrible mistake with Charles, who had been a pale imitation of the type of virile manhood that Jack showed, what kind of disaster could she create with Jack?

"Li-listen," she said shakily. "This is ... this is a really bad idea." She lifted trembling hands to cover her face, then peered at him over the tips of her fingers. "I'm not..." She paused as her eyes focused on the back of the shop where she saw movement.

"You're not what?" Jack demanded, lifting his hand to turn her face back to him. "Not ready? So you say, but that's not the way I see it. Not eager? You and I both know that's a lie."

Shakily, Mallory pulled her chin from his grasp, then twisted away from him. Fear had welled up in her—fear of her own feelings, of the sudden passion, of his strength and intensity.

Her greatest fear was of making another horrible mistake.

Because she didn't know what she should do about it, she lashed out as she lifted a trembling hand.

"Look," she demanded, her voice shaking. "There's your nephew in there with my little sister."

Jack's hands sprang away from her and he turned swiftly. At the door that led upstairs, T.C. stood with Sammi in his arms.

"That...that isn't right," Mallory stammered. "She's not ready for this. I've got to stop him." She started inside, but Jack grabbed her arm, holding her in place.

"He's only doing exactly what you and I were..." Jack's gaze shifted to her as his hand tightened on her arm. She could feel him willing her to look up. Unable to resist, she did so. "It's not Sammi you're worried about," he said harshly. "It's yourself."

Mallory stared at Jack for several moments, unable to think of anything to say. If she denied it, he would scoff. If she admitted it, he would sneer.

Instead, she lifted her chin and looked him straight in the eye. She could only hope that he couldn't see how her lips were trembling, lips that were still bruised from his kisses.

"Excuse me," she said. "I'm going inside to deal with a family problem." She reached for the doorknob, but his hand settled over hers.

"I'm coming, too. This involves *my* family, as well." His voice was hard enough to bend steel.

Mallory knew she couldn't stop him. "All right, come on in." She said it as if she was the one in control, but his firm hand on hers told her they both knew she wasn't.

"I'll come to make sure you don't do or say anything foolish."

"I don't need you to tell me how to deal with my own sister."

"No," he said, his tone ripe with disgust. "I've given up on trying that. But you do need me to tell you how to deal with my nephew."

Giving him a furious look, Mallory shoved the door open and strode inside. T.C. and Sammi sprang apart. The young man flushed guiltily when he saw Mallory and his uncle, but he stood up straight and met their eyes steadily.

Mallory chanced a quick glance at Jack and saw that his expression wasn't the wink-and-nudge one she might have expected, but was a man-to-man request for an explanation.

Confused, she looked at her sister and saw that Sammi's face was pink, flushed with joy as she gave T.C. an adoring look, then turned a happy smile on her sister.

"Hi," she said breathlessly. "Did you two have a nice evening?"

Mallory's heart thumped painfully in her chest and sickness twisted her stomach. Seeing her little sister's rapturous expression made her feel worried, unsettled and jealous all at the same time. She was about to answer when Jack took over.

"We had a fine evening. How about you?"

"It was wonderful. T.C. came over to watch a movie with me on television. We had popcorn." Her voice was so full of delight, she could have been relating the events of an evening spent in some wildly exciting pursuit. "Then he took me out to his house to see the new colt they've got."

"I...I saw it, too," Mallory said.

"Isn't he wonderful?" Sammi asked, sighing. Without a hint of self-consciousness, Sammi reached out and slipped her hand into T.C.'s. He gave her a startled look that quickly switched to pride. His big fist closed around her hand and the two of them stood shoulder-to-shoulder facing Jack and Mallory. He might be only twenty years old, but he was a man and he knew what he wanted. Obviously, a family trait, Mallory thought in despair.

Something twisted inside Mallory. She felt almost as if her sister was united with T.C.—against her. She wanted to pull Sammi upstairs and warn her against what was happening. Sammi wasn't ready for the kinds of emotions that Mallory could so clearly read on her face. And yet, would Sammi listen? Mallory herself hadn't listened when her parents had tried to warn her about self-centered Charles Garrison, and she had supposedly been more mature than Sammi was at the same age.

Against her back, she could feel Jack's unyielding presence. The force of his will was telling her that he was watching her carefully, ready to jump in and stop her if she said the wrong thing. Telling herself that she wasn't doing this to satisfy him, she managed to summon a smile for her sister and say, "That sounds like fun, but it's getting late and we have to work tomorrow, so—"

"I'll be going," T.C. broke in.

"I'll walk you to your Jeep," Sammi quickly offered.

The two of them had to squeeze past Mallory and Jack in the store's aisle, and in the ensuing shuffle, Jack pulled Mallory against him and held her there until they were alone.

When the other two were outside, Mallory jerked her arm from his grasp and turned on him furiously. "It's nice to see that one member of your family has some manners. It's time for you to go, too.''

Jack's strong features became harsh in the dim light. "You didn't seem to mind my manners too much outside when you were trying to crawl inside my skin.''

Mallory's lips tightened and turned down at the corners. "That's disgusting.''

"It's a fact.''

"You're . . . you're just angry because I turned you down. I wouldn't go back to your place with you, and . . . and—''

"You would have gone, Mallory," he assured her in a tone that made her think of the low growl of a very dangerous animal. "If you hadn't let your fear get in the way of your good sense, you would have gone.''

"Don't flatter yourself." She was recovering from her shock now, regaining her composure. With sheer bravado, she tilted her head and gazed at him.

"I don't, Mallory." He stepped so close that she thought for a second he was going to take her in his arms once again. If he did, she wasn't sure she had the will to resist him in spite of her defiant words. "I never flatter myself. The way you kissed me outside is all the flattery I need.''

She gritted her teeth, knowing she had surely lost this argument. She could deny it all she wanted, but they both knew the truth.

Mallory was buffeted by such a mixture of emotions that for a moment, she couldn't pick out the one that bothered her the most. She finally settled on betrayal. Jack Clanton had fooled her once again. He had spent the evening posing as the most amiable of men, a charming and knowledgeable companion who teased and followed her lead in conversation. How could she have forgotten that he had a basically relentless nature?

"It's time for you to go," she repeated.

Jack lifted his hat and resettled it on his head. He watched her from beneath the brim. She tried to hold his gaze even as she wished he would go away and leave her alone. Sammi would be coming back any minute now, and Mallory needed to think what to say to her.

Jack was having none of that. Instead, he said, "What was so terrible about your marriage that it's made you bitter enough to begrudge your own sister some happiness?"

"I don't begrudge her some happiness," Mallory hissed.

"What was it like?" he cut in.

"That's really none of your—"

"What was it like?"

She glared at him, then blurted, "Charles was jealous."

Jack crossed his arms over his chest and looked so superior that she wanted to shove him. "Did you give him reason to be?"

"Ohhh... you're so smug. You think you know everything and you know nothing!"

"So tell me."

"Charles wasn't jealous of other men," she spit out furiously. "He was jealous of knowledge. Whenever I delved into any subjects on which he considered himself to be an expert, he degraded my research, my conclusions, everything. He always had to be right. He could never admit when he was wrong.'' She fixed him with her fiercest glare. Her pride wouldn't let her admit that her discussions with her husband had usually ended with her near tears and Charles triumphant. ''And yet, the most ironic thing was that he wrote two books on Western history and I did the research, the typing, even much of the first draft.''

''I heard that when you were talking to him on the phone.''

She nodded. ''But all the ideas, the conclusions had to be his. The books have been published. The first one shortly after our divorce, the second a couple of months ago.'' She smirked. ''He sent me autographed copies.''

''But none of the money, I suppose?''

''Well, no. I had my divorce settlement and I wanted nothing further from him.''

''You were entitled to some of the proceeds,'' Jack insisted.

''No.''

He made a deep sound of disgust. ''You're saying you were a glorified secretary.''

''Not even glorified.''

''Why did you stay with him?''

Her glance darted around the shop, skimming over the neat displays, the carefully arranged merchandise, as if searching for the answer. ''I couldn't admit I'd made a mistake. My parents tried to tell me that he was too old for me, that he was self-absorbed, that it wouldn't work out.'' Mallory turned anguished brown eyes on him. "It...it wasn't always bad."

"Only when you tried to think for yourself, have your own life and interests," Jack concluded. "Like having your own business."

"And bringing Sammi to live with me."

Mallory knew she was saying too much. All the emotions she'd felt that evening were crowding in on her, from the warm companionship they'd known at the beginning to the wild desire they'd experienced outside her door. She was in overload like a circuit with too many conflicting currents running through.

Jack stared at her as his hands slowly closed into fists. "The jerk didn't like Sammi, did he?"

She shook her head. "When I wanted to bring her to live with us so Mom and Dad could accept the Peace Corps posting, he refused, said she should be in an institution."

Jack swore low and savagely under his breath. A flush of furious red ran beneath his skin. "And that's when you left?"

"Yes." Her shoulders were stiff, straight.

"Was that why he called the other day, to see if the two of you had fallen on your faces yet?"

"That's right. I think he's gotten it into his head that I might come back." Mallory shook her head, then pushed her drifting hair out of her face. "I can't imagine why he thinks that. We hadn't talked for months."

"He wants something."

She shrugged. Her emotions were too raw to go on with this talk, and Sammi would be returning any minute. She didn't want her little sister to find her upset like this.

Jack's eyes were dark and as hard as jade. "You think T.C. is going to treat Sammi like that? That I'm going to treat you like that? That every minute of your life will be a struggle the way it must have been with that creep Garrison?"

Frustrated, Mallory pressed her hands against her head. "Jack, I don't want to talk about this. This isn't getting us anywhere—"

"Because you won't let it!" He whirled around, paced a few steps, then circled back to her. "Do you know why I told you about my family, Mallory?"

Dropping her hands, she shook her head warily. "So you'd know what to expect from me."

"That'll be a first! I haven't known what to expect since the moment we met."

"I explained about my family so you'd understand that I'm a self-made man in the old-fashioned sense of the word. I don't let things stand in my way for very long. Not poverty, not abandonment, not a stubborn woman."

Mallory's hands closed into fists at her sides. "Thank you for the warning. I'll be sure to avoid you from now on. Why don't you go away?"

His jaw hardened and he raised one hand as if he'd like to shake her. Instead, he pointed a finger straight at her nose.

"I'll leave now, Mallory, but I'll be back. I'll be seeing a great deal of you. This is a small town. I'm renovating your house, and like it or not, my nephew is falling in love with your sister. And she's falling right back. Oh, yes," he murmured, his voice low and intimate in the dimly lit shop. "I'll see you day after day and on one of those days—and I promise you it will be soon—you'll realize that I'm nothing like your ex-husband."

"Jack, this is all going so fast. I can't think...."

"Think about this." He stepped to her, closed his hand over the back of her head, and placed his mouth over hers. He was bold and demanding. His mouth was warm, welcoming, beckoning her to delights and pleasure she could only imagine.

Oh, Lord, how could it be like this? How could she feel everything so keenly when she never had before tonight? If the experience was so new, so painfully intense, how could it feel so right?

He pulled away, but forced her to tilt her head up and meet his eyes. "Don't be afraid."

"I'm...I'm not afraid of anything," she bluffed.

He gave that statement the credit it deserved by ignoring it altogether. He wrapped his hands around her shoulders, cupping them with enough force to keep her in place, but not enough to bruise her. "It's going to happen between us someday, Mallory. Why don't you just get used to the idea and stop all this dodging and weaving?"

Somewhere her common sense was insisting that she should end this conversation. She could simply turn around and walk upstairs, leaving Jack to find his own way out and Sammi to lock up. That probably wouldn't happen, though. Jack would stay right here, holding on to her until he got the answer he wanted. She couldn't give in to him so she struggled on. Her dark hair drifted around her shoulders as she shook her head. "You said you weren't interested in marriage."

"Mallory, you're jumping the gun. Who said anything about marriage, which you told me you think is a trap? We've barely had our first date and our first kiss."

"You wanted more," she accused. "You said so yourself."

"That doesn't mean I would have forced you into anything." His eyes mocked her, but his voice was heavy with promise. "I'm not him, Mallory. I'm not like him. The reason he hurt you was because he didn't value you. It's not that way with me. There can't be anything between us, though, until you're honest with yourself. Just remember, Miss Earp, that we Clantons are a pretty persistent bunch. That goes for my nephew. And for me."

He gave her a confident nod and strode out the door, leaving Mallory with her stomach doing a fast dive toward her shaking knees.

Mallory walked the perimeter of her new home, her booted feet kicking stones out of her path as she went. The early-morning sun slanted its bright rays around her and a spring wind sent gusts spiraling up the small canyon behind her.

She was dressed in a red silk baseball-style jacket and faded blue jeans that she'd kept tucked away during the entire six years of her marriage because Charles hated jeans, dubbing them unfeminine. Her hair hung down her back, but she ignored it when the wind twisted and tangled it.

Pulling her hands from her pockets, Mallory pressed her fingertips against her eyes, hating the exhaustion she felt, hating even more the knowledge that it was her own fault.

She rolled her shoulders, trying to ease out the tension that had settled there, then huddled into her jacket and turned to examine the progress that was being made on the house.

She was glad to be alone on the small mesa that faced the hometown she had chosen for herself.

No one had come to work yet and it was just as well. Mallory had come to the house to be alone before she had to open her shop and face her sister.

The roof was completed over the main part of the structure and the frame was up for the bedroom and bathroom addition. It would be done in less than a month and she was sure she and Sammi would be very happy there.

That is, if Sammi ever spoke to her again.

Mallory groaned at the memory and then restlessly began wandering the length of her property.

She had made an absolute fool of herself last night. She had done exactly what she had promised herself she wouldn't do—what Jack had ordered her not to do. After Sammi had returned from seeing T.C. to his Jeep, she had insisted they have a talk.

It had not gone well.

Sammi may have been developmentally delayed and protected from harsh reality, but she knew the facts of life. She had very calmly told Mallory that she was in love with T.C. and nothing her sister said could change her mind.

That was the point where Mallory had heard echoes of her own protestations to her parents that Charles was the man for her, that she would love him and be happily married to him for the rest of her life.

Recalling that bit of idiocy, Mallory grimaced. Sammi simply didn't know what she was getting into. While it was true that T.C. was nothing like Charles, Sammi didn't know him well enough to say she loved him. When Mallory had pointed that out last night, her sister had lost her temper. Since that had rarely happened before, Mallory, already upset from her confrontation with Jack, had over-reacted. She and Sammi had gone to bed angry. After a sleepless night, Mallory had risen early and come up to the house for some time alone.

She turned and walked past the piles of adobe block and entered the front door, where she was greeted by the scents of fresh plaster, paint and sawdust. Automatically, she made her way to her favorite spot, the window seat overlooking Tombstone.

She sat down, then had to grab for the sill to steady herself on the warped board. It was looser than ever, probably in preparation for being replaced. She scooted back carefully, lifted her boots up, and snuggled into the corner with her long legs forming an arch in front of her. Letting her head fall back, she closed her eyes.

Because she was tired, or so she told herself, her thoughts drifted to Jack and what he'd told her last night. She couldn't say that he'd tried to fool her. After all, she'd glimpsed that ruthless streak of his the first evening they'd met. However, he usually hid it behind his teasing, friendly facade.

Last night, the mask had been off. There was no way now that she could fool herself into thinking that there was anything resembling a boss/employee relationship between them, not that there ever had been. Nor could she fool herself into thinking that their teasing rivalry over the old Earp/Clanton feud could continue.

Those kisses last night and the things he'd said had changed everything. She wished it had never happened because she didn't want to face what it meant—that she wasn't as in control of things as she wished. She realized, too, that she hadn't resolved her feelings about Charles.

If she sat calmly for a while and sorted out what had happened, she could deal with it. Without Jack's disturbing presence to confuse her, she could get her thoughts, her life—and Sammi's—back on track. As long as he wasn't around to distract her.

When she heard the scrape of boots against the tile floor, her eyes sprang open. She sighed. No such luck. Jack was coming in the door.

He was dressed in his usual jeans, a dark blue denim shirt that had seen better days, and a down vest. His cowboy hat was pushed to the back of his head, giving him a devil-may-care look that was belied by the sharp interest in his eyes as they swept over her. He was carrying his tool belt and a thermos of coffee. His eyes were full of deviltry as he dropped the belt beside boxes of plaster stacked against the wall and opened the thermos cap to pour out some of the steaming liquid.

"I thought that was your car outside. Checking up on the work in progress?" he asked. "Or trying to figure some way out of our agreement?"

She almost jumped to her feet to confront him, to deny his accusation. Instead, Mallory forced herself to remain seated. She was quite pleased with the way she turned her head and gave him a nonchalant look. "Good morning, Jack. I see you're in your usual outspoken, know-it-all mood on this lovely spring day."

His eyes gleamed at her. "Why change a winning formula?"

Mallory clamped her lips together and reminded herself it was too early in the day to lose her temper. "To answer your question, I am here to check up on the progress of my house. It looks great. Why would I want to back out of our agreement?"

He sauntered over to her and offered her the coffee. "To keep my nephew away from your sister. To keep me away from you."

The brew smelled wonderful, but she had learned better than to take anything from Jack. There were usually strings attached. "Don't be ridiculous. I'm not afraid of you." She shifted on the windowsill and felt the loose board rock beneath her.

"I know that, Mallory," he said. Uninvited, he sat down by her feet. The board squeaked and he moved cautiously to make himself comfortable, then took a deep swallow from his cup. He offered it to her, but she shook her head. Settling against the wall, he went on, "You're afraid of you."

She lifted her chin to a proud angle. "I believe we had this conversation last night and it was just as boring and pointless then."

Jack's green eyes narrowed. "Once again, our opinions differ. It's getting to be a habit." He leaned forward, crowding her against the roughly stuccoed wall. "But habits can be broken."

CHAPTER SEVEN

MALLORY fought against the familiar feeling of being overwhelmed by him, of scrambling for her mental footing. "Would you please move?" she asked haughtily, but the effect was spoiled when the last word came out a little breathlessly. She cleared her throat and tried again. "I didn't invite you to sit down."

He took another sip from his cup and watched her over its rim. "Ah, you're a hard woman, Mallory Earp. No doubt it's a family trait rising to the surface. Although it does seem to have skipped Sammi," he added in a thoughtful tone.

Mallory ignored his dig and said, "Please move, so I can stand up."

He looked at her for a few seconds as if he wanted to deny her request, but finally, he set the cup down and moved it out of the way, then surged to his feet. His sudden motion made the loose board shift. Mallory slapped a hand down to steady herself. The split halves of the board were forced together, catching her palm in a painful pinch.

"Ouch!" she yelped, jerking it away. Shoving her uninjured hand down beside her, she tried to lift herself up. Cold air swelled up from between the pieces of board, making her shiver.

"What's wrong?" Jack demanded, reaching for her. "What happened?"

Embarrassed, she shook her head and tried to bat his hand away. This action dropped her back down again and this time she was pinched on her bottom. "Oh!" She scooted around, attempting to swing her feet over the edge of the window seat, and felt the board crack beneath her. Her hands and feet flailed as she tried to rock forward.

Jack finally seemed to realize what the problem was, and, done with waiting for her to ask for his assistance, he simply reached down, grasped her around the waist, and pulled her up.

In an instant, she was on her feet, with his arm firmly around her waist. Her hand flew up to rest on his shoulder while she steadied herself.

"Are you hurt?" He drew her away, checking for injuries.

"Only my dignity," she muttered.

"What happened?"

She rolled her eyes at him in a look that said she wished he wouldn't ask, then nodded toward the window seat. "That board's cracked and it pinched my hand."

Immediately, Jack took it in his and began rubbing her palm. "Is that better?"

Mallory nodded and resisted the strong need to massage the other injured area. She cast him another quick glance, but saw only concern in his eyes. "When I fell back, it also pinched my..."

When she didn't finish the sentence, he stared at her in puzzled concern. After a few seconds, his face cleared and the concern changed to a teasing glint. She knew what was coming. "You're being unnecessarily modest about this, Mallory. In fact, downright Victorian.''

She knew that, but as usual, she wasn't acting like herself around him. ''Never mind.''

''Would you like me to rub it and make it better, too?''

''I said never mind,'' she snapped, stepping away from him. ''Even though it *is* your fault.''

''Mine? How do you figure that?''

''If you hadn't sat down on it, too, it wouldn't have moved.''

Jack's grin was unrepentant. ''If I'd known your cute little tush was in such danger, I never would have forced my unwelcome presence on you.'' He tilted his head consideringly. ''No, sir, I sure don't want you hurt. Ever since I first saw you in a pair of jeans, you've made me remember why God made women.''

''Now there's a sexist remark if I ever heard one!''

''No, an appreciative one.''

Mallory clapped her hands onto her hips. ''Just like all conversations with you, this one is getting nowhere.''

''We're getting somewhere. We were talking about that board. It wouldn't have split if you hadn't panicked.''

''It hurt!''

His lips twitched, but he didn't answer. ''I think there was more to it than that.''

''I wish just once you could accept what I say at face value and not try to find a deeper meaning behind it,'' Mallory answered wearily.

"What would be the fun in that?" Jack stepped closer to the window seat and reached for the board. As his fingers wrapped around the edge, Mallory remembered the cold blast of air that had hit her. When she told him about it, he said, "How can that be? The wall is solid adobe."

"I'm just telling you what I felt, Jack."

"Let's take a look. This wood needs to be replaced anyway." He pulled on the old board and half of it came up with a squeaking wrench of nails. Setting the board aside, he reached for the other half and pulled it up, too. "You're right," he said in a voice gone soft with surprise. "There's a hole here."

Together, the two of them leaned forward and examined the opening. Where there should have been solid adobe blocks, a rectangle, about eighteen inches by seven inches, had been hollowed out.

"There's something in there." In her excitement, Mallory forgot how irritating Jack could be and touched his arm lightly. "It looks like a box."

Jack nodded in agreement and reached inside. He sifted through settled adobe dust to locate the edge of the box. They quickly discovered that it was wedged too tightly to remove, so Mallory fetched a putty knife from his tool belt.

After much prying and scraping away of the dried brick, one edge of the box came up. Jack set it on the top of the exposed wall and ran his hands around the lid. When he tilted the box up to examine it, they heard a sliding sound inside.

"There's something in it." Mallory's voice rose with excitement.

"I know." He ran his fingers over the top. "This looks like an old ammunition box."

"Ammunition? You mean like bullets?"

"Yes, although the handle's missing from this one."

"Do you think it's got bullets inside?"

He lifted an eyebrow at her. "Who would bury ammunition inside a wall?"

"Who would bury *anything* inside a wall?"

"The man who built this house."

"Your grandfather? Why would he have done that?"

"I don't know."

"Anything about it in your family folklore?"

"If there had been, it would have been found long before now."

"Oh, of course."

Jack tugged at the edge of the box, but it wouldn't budge and his hands went still, resting on the top. "It sure looks old enough to have been here since the 1920s." Stretching upward, he shoved his hand into his pocket and pulled out a pocketknife. He flipped out a blade and ran it under the edge of the lid.

Flakes of rust sifted down, but he patiently worked at the rim while Mallory's tension mounted. She didn't know why she found this so exciting except that she'd always loved old things with history, especially family history, attached to them.

After several minutes' work, Jack laid his knife aside and grasped the edges of the lid. Opening it without a handle to hold made it more difficult, but by twisting and tugging, the lid finally screeched upward.

Mallory's breath caught as the lid bent backward, revealing the dark interior. Jack reached in and pulled out an oilskin pouch.

"What in the world?" he murmured. Turning, he sat with his back against the wall and laid the pouch on his thigh.

"It's obviously something your grandfather wanted protected, but hidden," Mallory observed.

"No doubt." They looked at each other for several long seconds in shared anticipation, then Jack began folding the oiled cloth outward. The edges crumbled at his touch, but the inner folds were surprisingly supple.

Once the gray oilskin was open, they could see that it contained a folded paper with lines and symbols on it.

Heads together, Jack and Mallory puzzled over it until they realized that they were holding it sideways. Turned the right way around, it revealed itself to be a map of the Chiricahua Mountains. Military markings in the lower corner told them it was an old U.S. Army map made by surveying parties at the end of the last century.

"Jack," Mallory said, breathless with excitement, "this is quite a find, but why do you think he kept it in the window seat?"

"I don't know. What possible use could it be to him there?"

They studied it in silence for several more seconds until Jack gave a low grunt of surprise. His fingers tightened on the old parchment until his knuckles turned white.

"Well, I'll be damned," he muttered. "It's a map for finding Lying Jude's treasure."

"You're kidding!" Mallory made a grab for the map, but Jack held it away, still studying it.

His gaze, followed by his callused fingertip, ran swiftly over the lines and symbols as he noted the directions and cryptic messages written in smudged gray pencil.

"How did it get here?"

Jack hesitated so long that her eyes snapped up to meet his. "Mallory, I didn't tell you before, but George Early, the lawman who tracked Lying Jude Bluestone . . ."

"Yes?"

"He was my great-grandfather. He lived in this house with my grandfather, Jack, until his death."

Mallory stared at him for several seconds before outrage kicked in. "Why didn't you tell me this before?"

"I wanted to find out how much you knew, what proof, if any, you had that George hadn't found that bank robbery money and kept it. I was stunned to find out that you had his journal."

Sitting back on her heels, Mallory shook her head in exasperation. "So you filled me full of wine last night until I told you everything I knew."

His face was as hard as his voice. "You were very willing to talk."

"You're a low-down, dirty rat for tricking me like that."

"I had a good reason."

"Oh, sure." She made another grab for the map. "Let me see it," she insisted.

Jack's lips tightened in irritation, but he spread the yellowed document out so they both could see it.

It took several seconds for Mallory to calm down enough to focus on it. She felt hurt and betrayed, used the way Charles had always used her. She wouldn't react the way she had before, though. She would be calm and rational.

She examined the map, and after a few moments, she forgot her irritation with Jack because she was so enthralled by this discovery. Finally, she said with awe, "Lying Jude's treasure. I can't believe it. How...how do we tell exactly what all these mean?" she asked, pointing to the words.

"Some of them are topographic map symbols. You've probably seen some of them before. These lines indicate elevation. This V shows where a stream runs downhill."

Excitedly, she tapped a mark on the map. "Look. What about this X? That must mean this is the spot to dig for the treasure."

Jack gave her an amused look out of the corner of his eye. "Sorry to disappoint you, Mallory, but that just means it's a bench mark, or different elevation in the mountain range."

She didn't even try to disguise her disappointment. Her shoulders slumped. "Oh."

"You really didn't think it was going to be that easy, did you?"

"No, I guess not."

They examined the parchment together for a few more minutes. Her disappointment faded as her mind eagerly clicked over the possibilities this map represented. She couldn't believe this magnificent stroke of luck. She might be within days of finding the treasure if she could only decipher these strange symbols.

Jack didn't seem to be having much better luck than she was. He was frowning over the map, his thick brows drawn together in concentration. Temporarily distracted from the document, she studied the way his black hair fell over his forehead. Absorbed in examining the map, he didn't seem to notice it.

She was still angry with him, but to her dismay, Mallory found herself curling her fingers into her palm to keep from reaching up and tucking the strands into place beneath his hatband. Oh, Lord, this had to stop. Somehow she had to get this welter of emotions under control. Her absorption with him was turning into a full-time occupation.

His arm moved as he adjusted the map to a new angle and Mallory felt his warmth seep through her jacket and into her own skin. She marveled that such a simple act could have such a profound effect on her, making her recall the way he'd kissed her, the way his voice had deepened when he asked her to come home with him.

She felt shaken to her soul to realize that now, ten hours later, she wasn't sure she'd made the right decision.

Jack looked up suddenly. "I'm not sure about... What?"

Mallory felt heat rising in her face because she'd been caught staring at him. "Nuh...nothing." Quickly, she focused on the map and tried to recall what in heaven's name they'd been looking for. "Oh, um, none of this is very clear, is it?"

Heroically, she ignored the knowing grin on Jack's lips when he answered, "No, it's not."

"If X doesn't mark the spot to dig, what's the good of this map? How can we tell where Lying Jude's treasure is if it's not clearly marked?" She was quite pleased with the evenness of her voice.

She tugged on the document, and Jack finally surrendered it to her, sitting back to watch as she eagerly scanned it for some key to deciphering it. He reached over and tapped the penciled-in message. "We study this."

Mallory held it close and squinted. "I can't even *read* it."

"It would help if we had a magnifying glass," he admitted.

"I've got one at the shop." She started to her feet. "Let's go over there and look at it—"

"Wait. There are some things we can read." His finger tapped the message as he leaned closer. "These look like distances. See. 'Ten paces west, seventeen east.'"

"But from what point?"

"I can't tell that, either. We may need an expert to help us out."

"Do you know one?"

"Yes, Dan Wilkers. He's studied these things for years. Remember that he's a writer and researcher of Western lore with a special interest in mysteries and disappearances. He has a bad back that prevents him from going out hunting for them himself.''

"Do you think he'll help us read it?"

"Sure. He's my friend and he knows that George Early was my great-grandfather."

"Well, then he knows more than I did, doesn't he?" she asked. "Let's see him today."

Jack gave her a quelling look as he took the map and replaced it in its oilskin pouch, then he stared at her with narrowed eyes. "Have you ever seen a treasure map before?"

"Of course." Her fingers ran over the little pouch, trying to imagine the man who had put it inside the window seat. Why had it been so carefully hidden? Were the stories about Jack's great-grandfather true? Had he found Jude and kept the treasure for himself, possibly burying it for later retrieval? If so, why hadn't he ever gone back for it? She cast Jack a sidelong glance, wondering how much of this speculation she could tell him.

"What about one for this treasure?"

She looked up and frowned. It took a moment for her brown eyes to clear as she recalled what they'd been talking about. "Well, no, except for the few cryptic notes in George Early's journal."

"I think it's time I took a look at that journal." He nodded at the pouch in her hand. "It might make sense with what we have there."

Mallory hesitated. There was no reason why he couldn't, except that she was reluctant to surrender ownership of it. "I suppose so."

"It involves my family," he pointed out in a dry tone, obviously stung by her reluctance.

"So I hear. Why do you think he hid it in the window seat?"

"Safekeeping, I suppose. As I said, he lived here with my grandmother and grandfather. In fact, he was still alive when my mother was a little girl. He never lived down the rumors that he'd stolen the money."

Interested, and sympathetic in spite of herself, Mallory asked, "What did people think he'd done with it? I mean, if he'd found it, wouldn't he have left town with it?"

"The story was that he'd gambled it away. Remember, he didn't come out of the mountains for a while. People·said he had taken a detour by way of a high-stakes poker game and lost it all, then came home through the Chiricahuas and claimed never to have found it at all."

Mallory didn't want to care. Finding this treasure was as important to her as it was to him, but it involved a member of his family. She remembered what he'd said about his heritage. In the darkest days of his family's poverty, they'd had their heritage to help them hold on to their pride. The accusations against George Early had long been a sore point with his family, one he wanted to resolve.

"I want to use this map to clear his name," Jack said in a slow, even voice. "Today, the area looks much different than it did then, so I'll study it, then take it up to the Chiricahuas and see if I can pinpoint the area."

Mallory twisted around so she could look him right in the eye. "What do you mean 'I'?"

His eyes widened. "I thought you said you had a 'feeling' about where to look. You were going to hire a guide, remember? Are you saying you'd want to go with me?"

"Absolutely," she answered in a testy voice. "I've wanted to look for this for years, and I've got the journal."

"I've got the map." He plucked the pouch from her hands.

"Hey, wait a minute." Mallory tried to snatch it back, but he held it away from her.

Angrily, she lifted herself up and made a grab for it, but ended up sprawled across him. His arm shot out to encircle her waist and keep her in place. Mallory threw her head back and found that his green eyes were laughing at her. She tried to pull back, but his arm was like an iron band around her.

"It looks like we're at an impasse," he said, his tone full of humor at her expense.

"It looks like you're a jerk," she groused. "You don't know what it means to me to find that—"

"You don't know what it means to me," he shot back. "And worse, you're not even willing to think about it because you're too intent on what you want."

That stung because she'd just been having such sympathetic thoughts about him and poor old George Early.

She tried to move again, but he said, "If you don't quit wiggling around like that, I won't answer for the consequences."

She went still, but her lips pulled into a furious pout.

"That's better," he said.

"For you, maybe."

His grin flickered and he eased her away from him at last. "I suggest we form a partnership."

"What kind?" He allowed an inch of space between them and she took two, but his hand was very firmly planted across the small of her back, just under the hem of her jacket. The room was cold, the floor was cold, the wall beneath the window seat was cold, but that hand was warm and she felt it more than all the cold combined. She gave him a disturbed frown, cleared her throat, and said again, "What kind of partnership?"

"Fifty-fifty. We go look for the treasure together and anything we find we split right down the middle."

She propped her forearm across his chest, which, in spite of his down vest, was something like trying to get comfortable on a bed of iron, and tilted her head back. Her long hair spilled down over his hand. His gaze shifted from her face as he reached over with his other hand and lifted the loose strands from the dust-covered floor. He looped it behind her ear and held it, held *her*, in place with his palm cupping the side of her head. He was much stronger than she was. If he exerted the least bit of pressure, he could bring her down to meet his lips.

Mallory swallowed hard and tried to recall exactly why she had pushed him away the night before. It was hard to do so when she was on a direct eye level with his sculpted mouth and freshly shaven jaw, not to mention receiving a heady dose of his subtle, but potent after-shave. The combination was enough to make her insides quiver like gelatin.

Lord, how could a man look this good, smell this good, be this alert and challenging so early in the morning?

Because her heart was tap-tapping madly, she tried to cover it by giving him an ironic look. "Partnership sounds good, Clanton, but I've known you long enough to figure out that there's got to be a loophole somewhere."

"Ah, as I've said, you're a hard lady, Miss Earp. Maybe you just want to come along because you think I'll make a lucky find."

"Maybe."

"I can't promise you luck, and you're not interested in anything else I might offer." He let go of her suddenly and she nearly tumbled over backward.

Righting herself, she came up on her knees and stared at him. She felt embarrassed and anxious when she recalled the previous night. He had hit on so many of her fears, rattled the foundation of so many of her defenses, she was still shaken.

Standing, he reached out a hand and pulled her to her feet. "Take it or leave it," he said briskly as he swept her upward. "This is my only offer."

She knew it was a mistake to go with him, but deep in her heart she knew she couldn't resist the challenge. "If I come along, I want to be fully involved in the hunt."

He stared at her for a few seconds, his gaze dropping to her lips, skimming over her face, which was growing warm from his close regard, and coming back to meet her eyes. His voice was low and full of promise when he said, "Don't worry, you will be—as long as you remember that I'm the one in charge of it."

Mallory swallowed hard and licked her lips nervously. Suddenly she felt like a small animal that had built its own trap and blithely walked inside, inviting the hunter to shut the door. She cleared her throat and nodded decisively. "All right. I'll remember. Can we go talk to Dan right now?"

"Yes, and we'll stop at your place on the way and pick up the journal and the magnifying glass. Think Sammi can handle things at the shop by herself for a while? Because if not, I can get T.C. to drop by and—"

"She can handle it," Mallory said. "Let's go."

"You don't mind leaving today's work on your house unfinished?"

"You're a man of your word, Jack. I trust you to get back to it right after we talk to Dan."

His grin was unabashedly triumphant. "See? You *can* let go and quit trying to control everything. I think there's hope for you yet."

Rolling her eyes in exasperation, Mallory headed for the door at a quick pace while he strolled along behind her.

*   *   *

"This is going to be one for the record books," Dan observed as he sat back in his desk chair and viewed the two people sitting opposite him. "An Earp and a Clanton working together."

"Don't let it get out," Jack said with a glance at Mallory. "It might ruin my reputation."

Mallory smirked at him. "It can't get much worse than it already is."

Dan chuckled and sat forward to once again examine the map before him. The three of them had sat for an hour in his book-lined office with it spread out before them. They had compared locations and distances that were noted on the map with what was written in George Early's journal. They'd also compared it with a modern topographic map, which had so many squiggly lines on it, that to Mallory's mind it looked like a plateful of Chinese noodles. How were they ever going to find their way over ground that looked impossibly rough even on paper?

Jack didn't seem worried. He sat with his hands clasped loosely behind his head, his left ankle propped on his right knee, an expectant look on his face.

After a few minutes' silence, Dan looked up. "Okay, here's how I see it." Jack and Mallory sat forward eagerly to listen. "The notations on the map seem to make some sense with the information from the journal. Either George Early or Lying Jude Bluestone himself was trying to make sure the treasure would be hard to find."

"Whichever one it was, he succeeded," Jack said dryly and Mallory nodded in agreement.

"This may be harder than you two expect it to be," Dan pointed out. "You'll have to start here, in this canyon, and work your way up the sides of the hills. Rocks have rolled down and there've been mud slides all over this area for a hundred years. Even if you're in the right area, there's no guarantee that the treasure hasn't been washed down and re-buried. I'm afraid there's more chance of finding nothing than finding anything worthwhile at all."

Mallory looked at the place where Dan was pointing. It sounded like a daunting task. She could feel the eyes of both men on her. Dan's were sympathetic, but as usual, Jack's weren't. He probably expected her to throw her hands in the air and give up. Instead, she turned to him and said, "When do we leave?"

Respect burned in Jack's eyes and one corner of his mouth tilted up. "The weather's supposed to be good this weekend. Temperature during the day in the eighties and clear skies."

"All right. Let's do it." She stood and he joined her in preparing to leave. Dan refolded the map and handed it to Jack as she picked up the journal. They thanked him and he wished them luck as they headed for the door.

Within a few minutes, they were standing on the sidewalk in front of Dan's house. It was set back from U.S. 80, which bisected the town of Tombstone and was a busy thoroughfare to Bisbee in one direction and Benson in the other. Cars whipped by, reminding her of the large volume of customers her shop served on weekends.

The day was turning warm so Mallory looped her jacket over her arm and stood smoothing the satin thoughtfully beneath her fingers.

"Having second thoughts?" Jack asked.

"Not about the hunt," she said quickly.

"About the time, then? We'll leave on Friday after you close the shop."

She bit her lip. "But that will leave Sammi all alone to run things on Saturday, our busiest day."

"T.C. will come in and help her. He learns fast. He can do anything."

Mallory thought about what Jack had said last night and about her argument with Sammi. She owed her sister an apology. T.C. was a good man. He treated Sammi like a princess.

"Yes," she agreed, meeting Jack's gaze. "Sammi can handle things fine with T.C.'s help."

Jack tucked in his chin and looked at her in surprise before saying, "Do you have a sleeping bag?"

"Sleeping bag? No."

He tilted his head. "You say that as if you don't know what one is."

"Of course I know what one is," she answered huffily. "I've just never used one before."

"You've never been camping out?"

"Of course I have. Charles owned a motor home that we often—"

"Motor home." Jack said the two words with scornful laughter bubbling through his voice. "You've got to be kidding. That's like taking your house right with you."

"Which is the way I like it."

He shook his head. "Well, here's a news flash, honey. I don't own a motor home and I have no intention of borrowing one just for your convenience."

"I didn't ask you to."

"We couldn't get one close enough to where we're going anyway. We'll have to hike for miles just to get to the starting point." He lifted an eyebrow at her. "You do know what hiking is, don't you?"

"Of course," she said, but honesty compelled her to add, "though I haven't done it much."

"Charles didn't like that, either, hmm? Tell me, what *did* that oaf like?"

She was tempted to say his greatest joy was in belittling her, but she bit her lip.

When she didn't answer, he went on, "I can't believe you've never really been camping out."

"Well, you don't have to say it as if I've missed one of life's greatest joys."

"But you *have*." Jack rubbed his chin with his thumb while he regarded her. "And it looks like you won't be camping out this weekend, either."

"What do you mean?"

"It means we've got to change our plans. Wait here," he said, turning back to Dan's house. "I've got to ask Dan something."

Mallory gave him a puzzled look, but she leaned against the side of her car and waited for him to return.

Within a few minutes, he loped out the door and rejoined her. He dangled a key in front of her face. "It's all arranged. Dan and Susan are going to let us borrow their cabin. It's not very close to the area

where we need to go, but it'll be easier on you."
He grinned. "It's even got indoor plumbing."

Mallory was stunned into silence, but then she
gathered her wits and gave him a grateful look. "I
take back every unkind thing I've said about you,
Clanton. You're a real pal."

He pocketed the key and headed for his truck.
"Remember that when you see the cabin," he
advised.

CHAPTER EIGHT

ON FRIDAY, Mallory closed the shop, made her bank deposit, then climbed the stairs to the tiny apartment. She changed into her oldest jeans and a long-sleeved T-shirt, then she braided her hair so that it would be out of her face. Sitting on the side of her bed, she pulled on her brand-new hiking boots. She'd had to go all the way into Tucson to find a pair that fit her narrow feet. They'd cost a small fortune, but they were waterproof, and best of all, comfortable. She was sure she'd be able to keep up with Jack as they hiked through the mountains.

She stood and looked down at the boots with satisfaction. Jack would have nothing to complain about.

Mallory walked into the living room, where she had assembled all the things she would need. Now she looked at it dubiously, fearing she may have forgotten something.

Along with changes of clothes, her warmest pajamas, her toiletries and makeup, she had her favorite pillow and some extra blankets. Although it was June now, she knew nights in the mountains could get very cold and she didn't have a clue about the accommodations at the Wilkerses' cabin. She'd wondered all week about Jack's cryptic comment that she should reserve judgment on the cabin until she'd seen it.

She couldn't imagine that she'd forgotten anything because she had tried to think of all the things that she had needed when she'd gone camping with Charles. Jack could laugh all he wanted to, but it had been good to have all the necessities when she needed them.

As she was examining the contents of an overnight case, Sammi came into the room and perched on the only chair in the room that wasn't covered with Mallory's camping gear.

Mallory studied her sister carefully. The atmosphere between them had been better since she had apologized. Lately, the gentle sweetness of Sammi's expression had taken on a special glow. Mallory was certain it wasn't because of the satisfaction Sammi was finding in her work in the shop, but in her budding love for T.C. Mallory was prodded by a twinge of jealousy. This business of falling in love seemed to be so easy for her little sister. Sammi was rushing into it with eyes wide and arms open. Mallory, on the other hand, was stumbling and fearful.

She looked up and smiled at Sammi. ''I think I'm ready to go.''

Sammi smiled her sunniest smile. "Did you say you were going to be gone for the weekend, or for the rest of your life?''

"It is a bit much, I guess, but I wasn't sure what to take.''

"Jack could have told you.''

"No doubt," Mallory murmured ironically, then gave her sister a hesitant glance. "Sammi, honey, do you think you'll be okay here alone?"

"Sure. Nobody's going to hurt me."

The perfect innocence in her face and voice tore at Mallory's heart. She came and sat down on the arm of the chair and gave Sammi a hug. After a moment, Sammi drew away and looked up at her, patiently waiting, Mallory knew, for her big sister to talk this issue to death.

She decided that, for once, she wouldn't do it. Sammi knew all about locking doors and setting alarms. They'd been over it enough times.

"T.C. seemed to understand how to write a sales ticket and use the cash register," she said.

"Sure. He's smarter than me."

Mallory's heart gave a painful lurch. It hurt to hear Sammi say that, but her tone was so matter-of-fact, she knew the girl wasn't feeling sorry for herself. "I don't think it's a matter of being smart. It's just knowing the merchandise and what people want."

"I learned that pretty fast," Sammi admitted with her usual candor. "But T.C. will learn quick, Mallory. You'll see." She tilted her head to the side and her lips curved into a knowing smile. "Why don't you just say what you're thinking?"

Mallory held out her hands, palms up. "I'm thinking it's easy for me to say you're ready to be on your own, but it's hard for me to actually let you do it."

"You sound just like Mom and Dad."

Sighing, Mallory dropped her hands. "And I swore I wouldn't."

"You think I'm a baby."

"No. No, I don't," Mallory rushed to reassure her, but Sammi broke in.

"I know I'm not smart, but I know some things," Sammi said, her mouth taking on an unaccustomed sullen look. "I know you think I'm going to be stupid over T.C. the way you were over Charles."

Mallory's mouth opened and then closed. How could she deny it? It's exactly what she'd been thinking for weeks. "It's true that I don't want to see you get hurt. Are you two going to get married?"

Sammi lifted her hands casually as if she was being asked about going out for an ice-cream cone. "Not yet. We want to be in love for a while first."

Mallory burst out laughing. "You think love will disappear once you're married?"

"It did for you."

"T.C. isn't like Charles."

"Exactly."

With a laugh, Mallory stood and kissed her sister's cheek. "I was wrong and I admit it. Go ahead, be in love, get married, be happy."

Sammi gave her a satisfied nod. "We plan to. I know we'll be good at the marriage thing."

"You're right about that," Mallory said. "T.C. is a fine young man from a good family. He's smart and hardworking, and I know he'll take good care of you."

Sammi gave Mallory an exuberant hug. "Thanks, Sis. You'll see, everything's going to be all right. T.C. will help me and take care of me and Jack will take care of you."

Mallory drew back. "Oh, honey, it's not like that between Jack and me...."

"Well," Sammi said in her guileless way, "it should be."

Mallory was thinking up another denial when she heard Jack's truck roar into the alley below their living-room window. He blew the horn to get her attention, then turned off the engine. She heard the truck door slam as he jumped from the vehicle and started for the back stairs.

She didn't have to look at Sammi to know she had a smug smile on her face as she hurried to the door in response to Jack's knock.

He entered with a wink and a wave for Sammi, who grinned back. "T.C.'s downstairs, Sammi," he said. "He drove over in the Jeep."

Sammi blushed and hurried for the door. "He said he'd take me to a movie," she announced with a quick glance at Mallory, who smiled back. "I'll see you Sunday, Mallory. Good luck."

In a rush, Sammi grabbed her purse and disappeared down the stairs. Jack walked over to Mallory and she forgot about her sister as she met his eyes. They were very bright and full of mischief as they swept over her, paused on her shiny new hiking boots, then lifted to her face. His generous mouth twisted into a grin that made her heart do a belly flop.

"I see you're dressed for action, Miss Earp."

Mallory felt pleasure settle inside her. Really, she didn't know why she felt this ridiculous surge of delight at seeing him. They'd probably end up fighting all weekend.

"I'm all ready," she agreed breathlessly, looking around for her purse. "If you'll take those bags, I'll get these, and... What's the matter?"

Jack stepped back and glanced around, obviously noticing the accumulation in the room for the first time. With an expression of utter amazement, he stood staring at the mound of bags she had prepared.

"Are you expecting to be snowed in up there?" he asked.

"Of course not." Her hands flew out. "These are all things I need. I wouldn't be taking them if I didn't need them."

Jack removed his hat, ran his hand through his hair, and resettled the hat on his head, looking at her sternly from beneath the brim. "We're going to be staying in a cabin that has all the necessities, then we're going to be hunting for lost treasure. We're not going to have time to attend a fashion show."

"Yes, Jack, I know that," she answered patiently, though her teeth were gritted. "But I'll need clean clothes." She broke off and stared at him. "Don't tell me you're not taking any?"

"Well, not my whole damned wardrobe. Two changes should be enough."

Jack picked up a duffel bag, unzipped it, and began dumping the contents on the sofa. Lacy underthings spilled out haphazardly along with thick socks, jeans and flannel shirts.

With a gasp of dismay, Mallory made a grab as a pair of panties went flying, but Jack was quicker. He snagged them in midair and let them dangle from one finger as he admired their pink silkiness. "Nice," he commented. "Very nice. Did old Charlie the jackass ever see these? If he did and he still let you go, he was an even bigger fool than I thought."

With a swipe of her hand, Mallory snatched them from him. She stuffed them down behind a sofa cushion. "Leave Charles out of this. In fact, leave my lingerie out of this altogether."

Jack's eyes lit up and he gave her a goofy smile. "Did I hear you right? Did you say for me to leave you out of your lingerie? Honey, isn't this a little sudden? I don't usually get offers like that until the third date."

"Oh, will you please stop?" she cried, trying to fight down the burning in her face as well as the need to laugh. "Can't you be serious?"

"That's what you don't understand about me, Mallory," he said with an unrepentant grin. "I'm *always* serious." He grabbed the bag he'd just emptied and folded two pairs of jeans, two shirts and some changes of underwear into it. "You can sleep in your clean change of clothes," he said, ignoring her gasp when he tossed out her warm flannel pajamas.

"I'd rather sleep in these," she insisted, stuffing them back into the duffel.

"Have it your way. I'm only trying to help." Then he rifled her toiletries next, tucking only the basics into her bag. "You won't need makeup," he pointed out. "No one will see you except me, and I don't care what you look like."

That statement stung, and because she didn't want to explore the reasons why, Mallory treated him to a venomous look.

In no time, Jack had what he considered to be her necessities packed into one small bag. He even refused to let her take the pillow and extra blankets she'd selected, saying they'd just weigh her down.

Finished with repacking her gear, he nodded in satisfaction, picked up the duffel, and handed it to her.

Mallory snatched it from him. "Now I fully understand why your ancestors in this town all came to violent ends. If they were anything like you, the Clantons must have irritated the daylights out of everyone they met, enough so that people wanted to do away with them."

Jack opened the door and waved her out. "Mallory, your compliments are just plain embarrassing. You're going to turn my head."

With an irritated huff of breath, Mallory swept past, locked the door, then hurried down the stairs. At the bottom, she was met with a sight she hadn't expected. A horse trailer was attached to the truck.

She turned and stared at him. "What's that?"

Jack made a big production of peering around her shoulder and giving the horse trailer a careful look. "Those are horses. I believe you've already met Garnet. I brought Turq for you."

"Turq?"

"Short for Turquoise. She's gentle as a lamb. You'll love her."

Mallory gave him a look that said she seriously doubted that. "You didn't tell me we were going on horseback."

"You didn't ask." Jack took the duffel and slung it into the back with the rest of their gear. "You do know how to ride, don't you?"

"Well, yes, but it's been a long time."

"Don't worry, it'll come back to you," he said as she climbed in.

"You said we were going to hike." She held up her foot. "That's why I bought these new boots."

He gave them an admiring look. "And lovely they are, too. Don't worry, you'll get your money's worth out of those, but we'll be riding some, too." He rounded the truck and was about to climb behind the wheel when he stopped. "Relax, you'll have the time of your life."

Mallory wrinkled her nose at him. "That's what I'm afraid of."

Jack started to laugh, but the sound was abruptly broken off when he looked over her shoulder at something near the mouth of the alley. Mallory glanced over her shoulder, then whipped around to stare.

"*Charles*? What are you doing here?"

"I came to visit you, darling, since you don't seem to have time to talk to me on the phone." He walked toward her, looking as out of place in his open-throated silk designer shirt and pleated slacks as a peacock in a henhouse. He stopped in front of her and examined her jeans and boots. "You look wonderful, if a bit rustic."

Too stunned to respond, Mallory simply gaped at him.

Not so Jack, who stepped forward and said, "What do you want, Garrison?"

Charles blinked and tilted his head to look at Jack. He wasn't a tall man. He and Mallory were the same height and Jack outweighed him by many pounds. Mallory glanced at the two men. Jack also outintimidated him by any measure.

"Do I know you?" Charles asked.

"Probably not," Jack answered, his tone barely a notch above contempt.

Charles's gaze darted to Mallory. "Where can we go to talk?"

"Nowhere," Jack said and crossed his arms over his chest.

"I wasn't speaking to you—"

"Why are you here?" Mallory interrupted.

"Obviously because I need to speak to you," Charles said in the falsely hearty manner she remembered all too well. But when he looked at her companion's glowering face, his expression grew uncomfortable.

"We were just leaving," she replied coldly.

Charles's face fell. "You're going away with this man?"

Jack took a half step forward, but Mallory laid a hand on his arm. "Not that it's any of your business, Charles, but yes, I am. For the weekend."

Her former husband drew himself up. "In that case, I'll speak to you about this matter right now, that is if your 'friend' will give us some privacy."

"Not a chance, Garrison." Jack stood directly behind Mallory's shoulder. In spite of her shock at seeing Charles, it occurred to her that she had never felt so supported in her life.

She lifted her chin. "Whatever you have to say, you can say right here and now."

Charles's lips pinched together, but he finally said, "All right. I need your help."

"With what?"

"My next book. I need a research assistant. You can work for me. Same terms as before."

Mallory's mouth dropped open. "Are you kidding?"

Charles took her question as a show of interest. He started to step closer, but Jack's icy glare warned him off.

"Yes, I knew you'd like the idea. I'll let you keep your little shop. Maybe you can hire someone to run it for you."

"You'll *let* me keep my shop," she choked out in amazement.

He smiled benignly. "That's right. How about if we start right away?"

Jack surged forward. "How about if I rearrange your—"

"Wait," Mallory said, holding his arm.

Jack glanced down. The shock in her eyes was making way for a healthy dose of anger. With an imperceptible nod, he stepped back.

Charles, oblivious to this byplay, must have thought he had gained her support. He allowed himself a small smile of satisfaction until Mallory said, "Charles, I have no intention of leaving my business and my new home to go back to being your underpaid ghostwriter. Research assistants are a dime a dozen. Why do you need me?"

"We work well together. You were willing to take direction, and—"

"She's not anymore," Jack broke in. "She asked you a straightforward question. Why do you need her?"

Jack's aggressive speech shocked Charles into an honest answer. "My editor says unless I can come up with a better first draft, he won't give me a contract for the book."

Jack made a sound of disgust and Mallory shook her head. "And I was fool enough to write the first drafts of the last two. No, Charles, I won't do it. For this book, you'll have to sink or swim on your own."

She left him squawking in protest and turned to the truck. Jack was right here to help her in. "Good girl," he murmured and she shot him a grateful look.

He slammed the door shut and started around to his own side. Charles rushed up and grasped the open window.

"All right, all right," he called out in panic. "We'll go fifty-fifty on the money. I'll even put your name on the cover as co-author."

She gave him a disgusted look. "No, thanks. I've had a better offer." Reaching out, she grabbed the handle and cranked up the window.

"What better offer?" Charles yelled.

Jack stepped close to him and spoke in a voice too low for Mallory to hear. Whatever he said made Charles blanch and stumble back, but when Jack started around to the driver's side of the truck, Charles lunged for her window.

"Is what he says true, Mallory? That you're his now? Is that the better offer you've had?"

Mallory's gaze flew from Charles's furious face to Jack's satisfied one. He gave her a look that dared her to deny it.

Deciding she would deal with him later, she rolled the window down a crack and called out, "My better offer is that I'm going to find Lying Jude Bluestone's bank loot. Remember the one you said doesn't exist? I've got proof!"

Jack started the engine and put the truck in gear. They rolled forward, leaving Charles sputtering in rage as they pulled out of the alley and onto the street.

The drive into the mountains took a slow two hours. It took Mallory the full time to calm down. She was appalled at Charles's nerve. He was so arrogant and self-absorbed that he'd honestly thought she would leap at the chance to give up her new life and return to him.

She considered it the height of irony that he had belittled and denigrated her ideas and her work, and now he couldn't do without her.

At one point in the ride, she turned to Jack and said, "You were right. He did want something."

Jack answered with a swift glance that took in the outraged color in her face and the fire in her eyes. "Told you," was all he said, but he turned back to the road with a thoughtful expression.

Mallory took a deep breath. She was going to have to talk to Jack about what he'd told Charles—that she was his—but it would have to wait. She'd had enough shocks for one afternoon. She sat back and looked out at the mountain. Pine trees edged right up to the pavement, but behind them were rocks, huge granite boulders stacked and tumbled together as if a giant hand had taken a swipe and knocked them around.

Although she'd read a great deal of literature about these mountains, she'd never been here before. Viewing the enormous boulders, though, she could see how easy it would have been for the Apaches to elude the horse soldiers for so long— or for Lying Jude and his stolen money to disappear. The road wouldn't have been a well-paved highway such as this one, but a narrow track in the places where there had been any road at all.

The drive began to calm her. Mallory leaned her elbow on the windowsill, rested her chin against her knuckles, and thought about the past few weeks. Even though she had expected that the challenge of running her own business would be tough, and watching out for Sammi would require patience and understanding, she'd thought her life would move along smoothly and calmly for a while. Living in a small town was supposed to be easier, or so she'd thought. No one had warned her that men like Jack even existed, much less would be a threat to the peaceful life she'd planned.

It was disconcerting to realize that she felt more alive than she ever had before. In her whole life, she had never laughed so much, been so angry, or argued as often as she had since meeting Jack— and never had she felt as supported as she had today when facing Charles, in spite of Jack's final outrageous statement to her ex-husband.

It was exhilarating, but frightening because it would be so easy to let herself depend on Jack. She cast a sideways glance at him, noting the casual way he held the steering wheel, with one elbow propped on the open window. He had qualities of dependability and endurance that she admired.

With a sigh, she turned her attention to the road. She felt as if she didn't know herself anymore, as if she no longer fitted into her own skin. It was impossible for her to know how much of that was her own fault and how much was because of Jack and his effect on her.

Her self-searching thoughts were disturbed when Jack stepped on the brake and, with a careful turn of the steering wheel, eased into a lane, which he followed for a quarter of a mile. At the end of it, he pulled into a wide parking area before a small, neat cabin.

"This is it," he said, switching off the engine.

Mallory stepped out into the quiet rush of the wind through the pine trees and stretched her legs. "It's peaceful here," she said, breathing in the crisp air.

Jack gave her a quick glance. "Not for long," he murmured in an ironic tone.

She turned and gave him a puzzled frown. "What do you mean?"

"You'll see."

"There you go with that Gary Cooper impression again."

He ignored her. "Here, help me with the horses." He led Turq out and handed Mallory the reins. She took the mare around to a small corral out back and Jack followed with Garnet.

Once the horses were settled with feed and water, Jack and Mallory returned to the truck for their gear. With their arms full, they made their way to the door, which Jack unlocked with Dan's key.

Mallory started to step inside, but he held his arm out to block the doorway. She looked up and he said, "Don't forget, I did this for your comfort."

"Did what?"

"You'll see," he repeated and pushed the door open, gesturing for her to step inside.

With a puzzled look at him, Mallory did so.

The cabin was just one big open room of about nine hundred square feet. It had a ceiling of exposed beams that were stained in a rich shade of dark mahogany. On one side of the cabin was a small kitchen area with a pine trestle table and benches. The other side of the room held two deep club chairs with hassocks and several small tables with lamps. Beneath a skylight in one corner stood a high double bed with a green plaid comforter for a bedspread.

Along the back wall was a door leading to a bathroom and one that appeared to open into a closet.

After a quick glance around, she looked at Jack, who was hovering in the doorway. "Why are you acting as if you're waiting for an explosion?"

"Because of that," he said, nodding across the room.

She looked where he indicated, then her eyes darted around the room. "There's only one bed," she said in a flat voice.

CHAPTER NINE

"THAT'S right. One bed." He pushed past her and deposited bags of groceries on the kitchen counter.

Mallory followed him and placed her own armload beside his, then turned on him. She crossed her arms over her chest and tapped her foot on the polished plank floor. "I wouldn't have come if I'd known there was only one bed."

He took a loaf of bread from one of the bags and laid it on the counter, then said, "I knew that. That's why I didn't tell you."

"And you probably made Dan promise not to tell me, didn't you?"

"That's right."

Facing him, she jerked up the sleeves of her shirt, spoiling for a fight. "I'm not sleeping with you, Jack."

He removed a package of cheese from the paper sack and laid it beside the bread, then picked it up and casually passed it from hand to hand. He kept his eyes on it as he spoke. She found herself watching the movement of that dark yellow brick as it moved smoothly back and forth.

"Mallory, you were married for six years. I don't think I have to tell you that there's a big difference between sleeping in the same bed with me and *sleeping* with me." His eyes came up to meet hers and his voice went low when he said the word.

His tone made her insides quiver with some kind of nameless anticipation. "I . . . I know that."

"I didn't bring you up here to seduce you."

Mallory ran her hands down her thighs and wondered when they'd begun to sweat. "Well, that's good, because that's not what—"

"We both know I could have seduced you right at home."

"In your dreams," she gasped.

With a bark of laughter, he tossed the cheese onto the counter and moved closer to her as he said, "And in yours, too, Ms. Earp. In yours, too." While she sputtered, trying to find a reply, he went on, "You can sleep with me or with the horses. It's up to you." Turning, he strolled outside and began gathering up another load of their gear.

Mallory glared at him. He had his nerve! All right, she would freely admit that she was attracted to him. When he'd kissed her, she'd nearly experienced a nuclear meltdown—not that she would ever admit such a thing to him. However, that didn't mean she would have gone back to his apartment with him as he'd wanted. She'd already proven that she was strong enough to resist him. She was simply choosing not to put herself in a tempting position.

"I can push those two chairs together and sleep on them," she informed him archly when he returned.

"That's up to you, but it doesn't look like a very comfortable arrangement to me."

"It'll be fine."

He gave her a look that said he didn't believe her, but he didn't reply as he began building a fire in the fireplace.

"A real gentleman would let me have the bed and sleep on the floor."

He was crouching before the fireplace and he turned with his forearm resting across his knee. "Honey, I was willing to sleep on the ground for you, but if there's a bed available, I'm using it. It's up to you to join me or not." He lifted both hands. "But if you think you can't share a bed with me and keep your hands off me, then go ahead and sleep on the chairs."

Her face heated up like a toaster, but she managed to give him a haughty look as she said, "Don't be ridiculous."

"Mallory, *I'm* not the one who's being ridiculous."

Fuming, she finished putting away their groceries and began dinner preparations for a simple meal of soup and sandwiches.

He didn't have to make it sound as if she was being petty and silly. She knew she was right. It was best if she ignored him.

By the time she had their simple meal ready and waiting on the pine table, she had calmed down.

Sitting down opposite Jack, she looked at the food and sighed. "You might find it hard to believe, but I'm actually quite a good cook."

Jack regarded her with more sympathy than she would have expected. "You probably had to be, as a faculty wife."

"Things are much different than they used to be. Most wives work now and many don't have time for the types of social activities that used to go on in academia."

"But Charlie expected it of you."

Because it was a statement without Jack's usual rancor behind it, she nodded. "Yes, and I was too young and naive to refuse."

Jack regarded her thoughtfully for a few minutes as if he wanted to say something, but finally, he nodded and began eating.

Mallory hesitated before picking up her own spoon. "Jack, thanks for what you did today."

He crumbled a couple of crackers into his soup. "I wondered if you would want to talk about it."

"Only to say thank-you." She shook her head. "I'm still amazed that he thought I'd jump at the chance to work with him on another book."

"*I'm* amazed you worked with him on the first two."

"So am I, now." Her deep brown eyes came up to meet his, then shifted away. "You shouldn't have said what you did today."

"That you're mine? Why not? It's true if you'll let it be."

"Oh, Jack, I—"

"But I'm a patient man," he said as if she hadn't spoken. "I can wait." He returned to eating, leaving her with her troubled thoughts.

Mallory breathed a silent sigh of relief. She should have felt reassured, she told herself as they finished their dinner and cleaned the kitchen together. He was really being quite a gentleman.

The only problem was that he didn't seem to fit into that role very well. He was a gentleman only when it suited his own purposes.

It was full dark by the time they'd finished cleaning up. They sat in the big easy chairs pulled up before the fire, but it wasn't long before Mallory was trying to cover her yawns.

Jack stood and stretched. "Why don't we go to bed?" Her eyes darted to him and she caught his quick grin. "Or maybe I'll go to bed, and you can go to, uh, chair."

"Thank you," she said sweetly. "You're so considerate."

"I've got to check on the horses." He grabbed a jacket from the rack by the door and went outside.

While he was gone, Mallory hurried into the bathroom, where she put on her pajamas and brushed her teeth. Returning to the main room, she whipped a pillow and extra blanket off the bed, then pushed the two big chairs together and climbed in to snuggle down for the night.

Instantly, she realized she'd made a mistake. Two pushed-together easy chairs were not long enough to provide a bed for a woman who was five feet nine inches tall.

However, she couldn't do anything about it right then because Jack was coming in the door. He gave her and her sleeping arrangements a disparaging look. "If you're not comfortable, you're welcome to join me."

She answered him with a bright smile. "No, thank you. This will be fine."

"Liar."

She stuck her tongue out at his back when he headed for the bathroom. As soon as the door closed behind him, she leaped out of her makeshift bed, added a hassock between the two chairs, and tried it again. Now she had an uncomfortable bump beneath her ribs and another under her knees.

She was just getting ready to try another arrangement when Jack came out of the bathroom with his shirt off and his jeans unsnapped at the waist. He walked to the bed and hung his shirt on one of the four posts, then sat down and began tugging off his boots.

Mallory glanced up and her mouth went dry from the desert heat that seared through her.

This was too much, she thought in despair. It was hard enough trying to keep her mind off him when he was fully clothed. This was too much.

His shoulders, which looked wide when covered by his shirt, seemed to block out all visible light when they were bare. Or maybe the blackness that was affecting her vision had to do with the fact that she was holding her breath. She exhaled quickly.

Hearing her, Jack glanced up, his green eyes catching the flickering firelight and reflecting a devilish gleam. ''You're sure you don't want to sleep over here?''

''I'm fine.'' Her voice squeaked and she cleared her throat. ''Just fine.''

He reached to turn off the lamp beside the bed. ''Good night, then.''

In the remaining light from the glowing fireplace, she watched him stand to unzip his jeans. Although she reprimanded herself for being nothing less than a voyeur, she couldn't seem to tear her eyes away as he slid them down his thighs and sat to tug them off his feet.

She saw the flash of skin, the startling whiteness of his undershorts, and heard the sliding whisper of the heavy denim being removed. Finally, she did what she should have done in the first place. She clapped her eyes shut and, turning away, did her best to ignore the uncomfortable chair edge beneath her rib cage.

After a moment, she heard the bed creak and all was silent. She listened for his breathing to become slow and even before she stealthily scooted onto her back. She moved her feet to one side and started to sit up, bracing herself with her hand on the chair where her head had been resting. The chair slid on the polished plank floor, shooting away from her.

She tumbled after it with a whoosh of breath and landed on her side with her feet tangled in the blanket.

"What the . . . ?" Jack's bare feet hit the floor with a thud as he shot out of bed. "Mallory, are you hurt?"

"Nuh . . . no," she gasped. "I'm okay."

Within seconds, Jack was crouching beside her. "I think the game of musical chairs is over for tonight, Mallory." Before she could protest, he reached down and picked her up, blanket, pillow and all, swinging her into his arms and striding back to the bed.

With one hand, he whipped back the covers, dumped her on the bed, then tugged her blanket from beneath her.

"You will sleep here, Ms. Earp. With me. You will not argue. You will not try to escape, hide, or otherwise keep me from sleeping. Are there any questions?"

Mallory kept her eyes firmly fixed on his face, which even in the dim light, she could see was none too happy. "Yes. Do you snore?"

With a harrumph of disgust, he climbed in beside her. "I don't know, but since you're so worried about your virtue, you can stay awake all night and listen. Tell me in the morning. Now can we please get some sleep?"

Mallory was enjoying his outrage. She turned away from him, tucked her pillow under her cheek, and smiled into the darkness. "Sure, Jack, whatever you say."

Mallory came awake slowly and feeling disoriented. The sun was coming from the wrong direction and she heard birds rather than the early-morning traffic at home on Allen Street. She was warm, too warm, with the weight of an arm around her waist.

An arm? She came to full alertness with a jolt, her eyes springing open. Jack had pulled her to him in the night, snuggling her close and making sure she stayed close. Besides his arm around her waist, his face was buried in her hair and one of his muscular legs was wrapped around both of hers. She felt as if the two of them had been sealed together.

While her body went stiff in surprise at the intimate contact, her mind kicked into immediate fantasies involving the two of them. She knew she shouldn't be enjoying this so much. She should wake him and insist that he let her go, and she would, too, in just a minute.

It had been a very long time since she had been in the same bed with a man. For the last year of her marriage, she and Charles had slept in separate bedrooms, and when they had shared a bed, he'd never held her like this.

Mallory closed her eyes again while her mind created pictures of her and Jack waking like this every morning, in the new bedroom he was already adding on to her house. Her fertile imagination couldn't resist adding to the fantasy—picturing them making love or being awakened by a couple of bouncy toddlers who demanded access to Mommy and Daddy's bed.

Mallory bit her lip, almost groaning aloud. Oh, this wasn't fair. She had worked so hard to keep from falling in love with him, but it seemed that all her barriers had been torn down in the one night when they'd done nothing more than share sleeping space. She couldn't let this happen, she decided. Restlessly, she moved her legs, trying to ease away from him.

"Be still," he mumbled, tightening his hold on her. He nestled his face farther into her hair and kissed the back of her neck. "You'll wake me up."

Oh heavens, she couldn't control the ripples of delight that shimmered through her, but she tried to keep her tone light. "If you're talking, you're already awake."

"I talk in my sleep."

She fought against laughing, against letting this feel too right and too secure. She couldn't fall in love with him.

Jack spread his hand over her ribs and massaged gently.

The shivers running through her were stronger than bolts of lightning. "Jack," she begged breathlessly. "Let me go."

"Uh-uh. I'm not awake yet and I can't make a decision until I'm fully awake."

"A decision?"

"About letting you go."

"You don't need to decide," she hissed at him desperately. "Just do it."

"In a minute." He moved his hand up to her shoulder and pushed gently until she was on her back.

Her deep brown eyes, dark and troubled, stared up at him. He was sleepy-eyed. His midnight-colored hair was tousled. His jaw was shadowed with whiskers as it had been the first time she'd ever seen him—and he looked incredibly sexy.

"Jack, please don't make this hard for me...."

"I'm trying to make it easy for you." His voice was low with morning gruffness, but his words were soft enough to melt her heart. "When was the last time you woke up with a man, Mallory?"

"That's really none of your business."

He cocked at eyebrow at her. "Honey, I have to tell you that prissy attitude doesn't work for you when your hair is tousled all over the pillow and your mouth is just begging to be kissed."

"The only thing my mouth is begging for is for you to let me up." She arched her body, trying to throw him off, but he just smiled and held her in place.

He ducked his head and feathered a kiss on the side of her neck. Mallory barely managed to bite back a moan of pleasure.

"Answer me, Mallory. When was the last time you woke up with a man?" This time he kissed her chin.

With a sigh, she surrendered, lowering her chin so that her lips were only millimeters from his. "A...long time. Almost two years. Since months before my divorce, in fact."

"Was there ever anyone else besides your husband?" He let his head drop so that she could feel him tantalizingly close.

"No. Never anyone until..."

Jack drew back, his green eyes dark and slumberous, but keenly fixed on her face. "Until what, Mallory?"

"Until you," she breathed, forgetting all the reasons she should insist that he get away from her.

Jack rewarded her with a kiss. He was warm and male, dominating and yet tender. Something inside her brain told her that she had been counting the hours since the last time he had kissed her. She didn't want to like it so much, like him so much.

Her mind teetered on the edge of accepting that she loved him, but she forced it to veer away, back into the safe zone of fighting her attraction to him.

She broke off the kiss and turned her head away. Longing warred with fear, but fear won. "Jack, please don't. I'm not ready for this..."

"Yes, you are." He used the edge of his hand to urge her face back to him. "Or you would be if you'd stop being afraid. Wyatt and Virgil would be awfully disappointed in you, Mallory. They, at least, never lacked for courage."

"They never had to face *you*."

He smiled then, a smile that was tender and yet edged with sadness. "You win, Mallory. I'll let you up if you'll give me one kiss of your own free will."

Relieved, she did so, a quick peck on the lips.

He looked thoroughly disgusted. "You call that a kiss? Garnet kisses better than that."

"Then go kiss her."

"She slobbers."

Mallory burst out laughing. "Yuck! What a thing to say."

"Oh, you think that's funny, do you? I'll give you something to really laugh about." Suddenly his fingers were on her rib cage, tickling and teasing. They found the particularly vulnerable spot just above her waist and she twisted and turned, trying to get away from him while she whooped with laughter.

"Jack, don't," she panted. Her stomach muscles were in agony from laughing and fighting for breath.

"Do you give up?" His wicked hands made a few more passes over her sides and she doubled up once again.

"Oh...okay. Okay, I—I...give up." Her breath came out in heaving sobs.

Jack pinned her down with his hands on her shoulders. "Now, do as I asked so nicely in the first place. Give me a real kiss."

"This is extortion," she complained, but her hands stole up over his shoulders. Her eager palms felt the warm smoothness of his skin, the firm expanse of his shoulders and the strong column of his neck. Her hands came to rest at the back of his head and locked themselves securely together.

"Extortion?"

"That's right. I should report you."

"Honey, you've said yourself that we Clantons are more familiar with the wrong side of the law than the right side."

"I'm going to have to reform you," she said, smiling up at him. Her face was glowing, flushed with happiness, in spite of the conflicting emotions she couldn't allow herself to express.

"Start now," he urged.

Mallory gave his head the gentlest of pulls and met his lips with her own. He didn't try to dominate the kiss this time, but let her take the lead.

Again and again, she touched her lips to his, tasting, exploring, wishing for more and more.

The sweetness of it was shattering. The promise she tasted and felt was enough to make her weep. The gentleness of his lips made her feel as if she was coming home from a long, dark journey. He was everything she wanted and needed.

Her old failures and insecurities stirred and lifted their tiresome voices. She'd made such a dreadful mistake before, for which she had paid and paid. Seeing Charles yesterday had made her recall how much she had paid.

Deep in her heart she knew, she *knew*, that Jack would never hurt her, but she was afraid to take the chance.

When the war between her desires and her fears became too much, Mallory drew back. Her smile was shaky, but she tried for a flippant tone. "There. Is that what you wanted?"

Jack's eyes lingered on her eyes, which were too bright, and her smile, which was as brittle as George Early's map. "It'll do for a start."

With breathtaking swiftness, he braced himself on his arms, rolled onto his elbow, then was on his feet. Quickly, he stepped into his jeans and pulled them up.

"We're burning daylight," he said, suddenly all business. "I'll start breakfast while you shower, okay?"

Even though it was what she'd insisted she wanted, Mallory felt deprived of his nearness. "That sounds fine, Jack." She hurried out of bed, gathered her clothes, and rushed into the shower. Since Jack had made her leave her makeup behind, her morning preparations took far less time than usual. She wasn't accustomed to seeing herself without at least mascara, and thought her face looked naked, but there was no help for it, thanks to Jack. She braided her hair and stepped out of the bathroom to the smell of perking coffee and frying bacon.

He glanced up with a swift grin that was full of casual friendliness. "Good girl," he said. "Finish this while I shower." He handed her a spatula, picked up his shaving kit, and headed for the bathroom.

Mallory stood holding the spatula and staring after him. Never had she known a man who could go from the verge of lovemaking to teasing humor and plain old friendliness with the ease Jack could. Not of course, that she'd known any man intimately except Charles, and she was quickly coming to discover that the two of them weren't even in the same universe of manliness.

The smell of bacon on the brink of burning alerted her to pay attention to her task. She turned it with quick flips of her wrist, then began making toast. By the time Jack emerged from the bathroom, freshly shaven and smelling heavenly, she had everything ready.

They ate quickly, washed the dishes, made some sandwiches for lunch, then headed out to saddle the horses. Mallory's excitement grew with each passing second. It was a wonderful morning. She was setting out to look for the answer to a mystery she'd been curious about for years. Gleefully, she pictured Charles's face when he learned of her triumph.

As she picked up Turq's reins and settled herself in the saddle, she looked over at Jack and grinned. "You were right."

"I usually am," he said with fake modesty. "But about what this time?"

"I'm having the time of my life, or at least I will be as soon as we find Lying Jude's bank loot."

Jack turned his head sharply, his eyes piercing in their intensity. Mallory's smile faded into a puzzled look, but he shook his head and led the way from the cabin.

"I don't think we're in the right place, Jack." Mallory frowned at the current topographic map Jack had obtained from the United States Geological Survey office and compared it to the map they'd found in the window seat.

"I keep telling you that you've just got to be patient. This area doesn't look much like it did a hundred years ago. It'll take us a while to find the right spot."

"At this rate, we'll be old and gray."

They had ridden for many miles into the mountains, over some ground that was rough and some that was so smooth it made riding a pleasure. As Jack had promised, Turq was a good horse, easy to ride and gentle-natured.

The weather was warm enough to make her glad she'd worn a short-sleeved shirt and sunscreen to protect her from the sun's rays.

Because they had dismounted and hiked several times in areas too steep for the animals, Mallory was feeling less saddle sore than she'd expected. She was also feeling less patient than she'd expected.

It wasn't that she thought Lying Jude's treasure would pop out of the ground and announce itself, but she'd hoped to at least have a clue by now that they were in the right area. They'd been out for hours, the sun had long since passed its zenith, and they seemed no closer to their goal than they'd been when they started out that morning.

They had taken several promising trails, but these had all led to dead ends or narrow canyons. So far, there wasn't a trace of the place their map indicated that they should begin pacing off their seventeen steps east.

For every wrong turn they'd taken, Mallory had felt as if they were getting farther and farther from their goal, rather than moving toward it.

With a frustrated sigh, she spread the maps out on a boulder and leaned over them. Jack, who'd taken the horses to a nearby stream for water, led them back, tied them loosely to the branches of a juniper bush, and came to join her.

"This is where we are now," he said, pointing to a small valley on the newer map. "But look at this." He placed the old map on top of it. "When my great-grandfather was chasing Jude through these mountains, this valley was much wider. It's just as Dan said. Rain, weathering, rock slides, all kinds of changes have happened here over time."

Mallory slapped her hands down on the two maps and spun away. "That means we may never find it." She paced across the rough ground, her arms crossed over her stomach, her fingers massaging her elbows.

Jack folded the maps, then sat on the boulder as he carefully tucked them into their pouches. He stood and stretched, then walked over and placed the two packages inside Garnet's saddlebag. He removed two of the sandwiches they'd made that morning and walked over to hand her one along with a bottle of water.

She started to refuse the food, but he said, "You'd better eat or you'll get light-headed in the sun. If you tumble off into a canyon, I'm not stopping to pick you up."

With a grimace, she accepted the sandwich. Moving back to the boulder, she sat down, unwrapped it, and took a bite. Jack crouched on one knee on the ground in a pose she'd seen in a hundred Western paintings and bit into his own sandwich, but his mind didn't seem to be on eating. He chewed and swallowed slowly, but his intent gaze was on her.

Finally, Mallory could stand it no more. "Do I have dirt on my nose, or have you decided you can't stand the sight of me without makeup after all?"

Jack took another bite before he answered. "You've been pretty anxious and pushy all morning. I know why I'm here, but exactly why are you here?"

CHAPTER TEN

MALLORY stared at him for a second. "I've already told you. This story has interested me for years...."

"But why, exactly?"

Her shoulders lifted swiftly, then fell. "I love history, you know that. That's why I own an antique shop. I helped Charles write his two books. I've done tons of research. Besides, it's a challenge to me, something I'd like to accomplish."

"Why?" Jack popped the last bite of sandwich into his mouth and washed it down with a gulp of water. "Why this particular one? Right now you seem a lot more anxious about it than I am."

She frowned at him, wondering why this sudden interrogation. Certainly, she had noticed that while she was becoming more and more distraught over their failure to find the right spot, he'd become quiet and watchful, obviously deep in thought.

"I told you, Jack, it interests me."

He rose to his feet and walked over to stand facing her. She had to tilt her head back to meet his eyes, which she could now see held an expression she couldn't quite read. It was as if he was waiting for her answer and didn't want to be disappointed.

"What made you become interested in Arizona history?"

"That's easy. My name, my ancestry."

"Is that what drew you to Charles Garrison? He's supposed to be something of an expert on lawmen of the West, and especially your relatives."

She tossed the remainder of her sandwich out for any interested wildlife and stood up. "Certainly we had that in common."

"And you? What drew you to Charles? I've met him, remember, and I can damned sure tell you it probably wasn't his personality."

"Jack, this isn't the time or the place to talk about my marriage."

"I think it is," he said, his voice low and steady. "After seeing that jerk yesterday, I know there's something going on in your head, something more than mere interest in Lying Jude's bank loot. You say it's a challenge to you, yet you just moved into a new town, opened your own business, and took over responsibility for your sister. How many challenges does one woman need? Isn't that enough?"

At a loss, she held out her hands. "This is different."

"Why?"

"It's of historical interest."

"Bull. There's something going on here or you wouldn't have such a knot in your tail about it."

"Oh, that's very elegantly put, Jack." She was beginning to grow angry. Why was he questioning her like this? As if her motives were wrong.

"Just answer me."

"Which question?"

"What made you become interested in Charles in the first place?" he asked in a patient tone.

"His knowledge," she retorted. "His sophistication. Oh, Jack, I was eighteen years old and away from home for the first time in my life. I didn't know what I was doing."

His eyes were sharp, but he nodded his head as if he understood and accepted that answer. "Okay, then my second question. Why this treasure? There are literally dozens of such legends and mysteries in the West. Why this one? Because Charles said it doesn't exist?"

Goaded beyond her limit, she snapped out, "That's right. Because no matter what proof I had, including the journal, he said I was a fool to pursue it. He was the expert, you see, and I was nothing but a research assistant. It didn't matter that I was also his wife. My opinion didn't count because it differed from his."

Her breath was coming hard, pushed by her anger and the sudden burst of words. She paused to get her breath.

Jack's face had gone hard, his jaw set as firmly as a bear trap.

"So this is all about proving yourself to your ex-husband?"

Stricken, she stared at him. "No, of course not." How could he think that? She'd been full of understanding about his need to clear his great-grandfather's name, to have pride in his heritage. Didn't he know she was doing this for him, as well?

"No, Jack, that's not true." She shook her head as she tried to come up with an explanation that would convince him. "If you'll just listen for a minute—"

"I've heard enough, thanks." He turned and glanced up at the lengthening shadows. "We'd better be getting back. We can try again tomorrow." He shot her a look that was both chilling and full of challenge. "We don't want you to go home empty-handed. That'll never do if you want to show up Charles."

"Now, Jack, that isn't fair," she flared, but he ignored her. Walking over to the horses, he took Garnet's reins and handed her Turq's. He swung into the saddle and started back the way they'd come.

Mallory scrambled onto Turq's back and hurried after Jack, fuming all the while. He was being unfair and he was refusing to listen to her explanation. Sure, she wanted to show up Charles, but there was nothing wrong in that. He had denigrated her ideas and conclusions so often during their years together that she felt perfectly justified in wanting to prove him wrong. However, it wasn't her only motivation for this hunt. She was concerned about Jack, too, and it peeved her that he believed otherwise.

They were silent on the ride home. Jack led the way back to the cabin, indicating direction to her by pointing. By the time they reached home, it was growing dark, and Mallory felt hurt, edgy and furious.

They brushed the horses down, gave them feed and water, then went into the cabin to prepare their own dinner.

Mallory would rather have been anywhere on

earth than in this cabin with the darkness pushing at the windows and the tense atmosphere inside.

The strain between them was as real as the dinner of chicken and baked potatoes they prepared together in the kitchen that seemed to be much smaller than it had the evening before.

They ate in further silence that seemed to have a life of its own, filling the room all the way out to its edges.

Mallory dreaded bedtime. She didn't want to lie on the same bed with someone who misunderstood her so badly, who thought she was shallow enough to want a form of revenge against Charles. Didn't Jack understand she'd had that satisfaction yesterday? Proving Charles wrong would be like icing on the cake.

They sat before the fire, both deep in their own thoughts. Mallory couldn't help stealing glances at Jack, wondering what he was thinking, wishing he would listen if she tried to explain.

He was sitting low in his chair with his long legs stretched out before him. The heel of one boot rested on the toe of the other and he seemed to have nothing else in mind but spending the evening looking at his own feet.

Frustrated, she stood and moved around the room, finally pulling her flannel pajamas from her duffel and heading for the bathroom. She changed into them, then stood before the mirror brushing her long hair out until it crackled and shone as rich as brown silk.

Realizing she'd put it off as long as she could, she reentered the main room. Jack was kneeling before the fireplace, banking the fire for the night. He stood and turned to her as if he had something to say, but then closed his mouth and walked past her.

Mallory swallowed the lump of dismay that formed in her throat, then moved slowly to the bed, lay down, and pulled the covers over her. Hugging her pillow, she tried desperately to think of something to say to him.

Before Mallory could come up with anything lucid, she heard Jack approaching the bed. Her heart stopped and she closed her eyes in misery when she heard him removing his clothes. He climbed into bed and she imagined him presenting his broad back to her.

There had to be some way to make him understand. Mallory decided to try one more time. She rolled over and laid her hand on his bare shoulder. The muscles tensed like steel bands beneath her palm.

"Jack, please listen to me...."

He flipped over in a surge of strength that took her by surprise. Placing his arm across her, he said, "No. I've listened enough. I've been patient enough. I've done every damned thing I can think of to make you forget him, except make love to you to wipe him out of your mind."

Her heart stuck in her throat. "Jack?"

His hand came up to cup her face, lifting her mouth to his. "I'm not going to be patient anymore, Mallory. I'm not giving you any more understanding, any more space. I'm going to make love to you. If you don't want it, say so now. It's your only chance."

Mallory was too stunned to form an answer. She stared at him, her eyes shadows in the darkness. In the dying firelight, she could see his face, full of determination and something close to pain.

"I want you like I've wanted no other woman in my life, Mallory Earp. If you don't want me just as strongly, tell me no right now."

Her hand trembled on his shoulder. "Jack, I—"

"Tell me no," he demanded.

Her mouth went dry and her tongue edged out to moisten her lips. His gaze went from her lips to her eyes, compelling her, showing her the direction her own will wanted to take.

"I . . . I can't tell you no, Jack."

Triumph came and went in his face as swiftly as lightning in a summer storm. With a guttural sound of deep satisfaction, he fitted his mouth over hers.

Mallory was transported back to the blissfulness she'd known that morning. Her arms flew around him, locking him as close to her as possible. His hands moved the length of her spine, lifted the hem of her pajama shirt, and kneaded her skin.

Mallory's breath stopped and she thought her heart had, too, before it started up again at a thunderous pace.

Jack's hands and his mouth were everywhere, bringing her intense joy, showing her the true meaning of passion.

He drew back once and his eyes glittered down at her with a fierceness that made her shudder.

"Tell me you're not thinking of him, Mallory."

He meant Charles, but she wouldn't speak the name because it would spoil everything.

"No," she whispered, kissing him. "There's only you, Jack."

"Good. That's the way it's going to be from now on. I was telling old Charlie the truth. You're mine now." He lowered himself to her and Mallory had no more thoughts except of him.

Mallory was awakened the next morning by Jack slipping from the bed. "I've got to see to the horses," he whispered, his voice low and gruff. "Sounds like something's got them spooked." He pulled on his clothes and his boots and strode outside.

Mallory heard the animals quiet immediately, though their stamping about and snorting hadn't awakened her. It wasn't until she'd felt Jack leave her side that she'd come fully awake.

She turned onto her side, blinking sleepily, and smiled. She felt as if she'd passed some impossible barrier. The circumstances were the same. She and Jack were still in the mountains, in the same cabin. They had spent the night in the same bed, and his arm around her waist and his leg crossed over hers had manacled her to him as securely as if she were bound by chains.

And yet everything had changed. She had made love with him and now she felt bound to him as she never had to her ex-husband. She had never responded to Charles as she had to Jack. In fact, there was no comparison whatsoever between them.

For weeks, Mallory had fought against the inevitable, but it had done no good. She was in love with Jack. It wasn't at all like the pale infatuation of youth she'd felt for Charles.

She realized now that if Charles hadn't encouraged her, certainly the most appropriate course since he was her teacher and so much older, her feelings for him would never have progressed beyond respect and admiration.

The love and emotional involvement she felt for Jack were so intense they were all-consuming. She wasn't sure how to deal with this, especially since she didn't know if he loved her. He said he wanted her, but that was no guarantee of love.

Mallory stretched, then curled into a ball and pulled the covers up around her head to block out the cool morning air—and thought about the man she loved.

She had never found it easy to read Jack. He could be teasing and serious with equal ease. He had certain strong beliefs about hard work and the importance of family—ones she certainly agreed with.

When he had been abandoned by his parents—one by desertion and one by death—he had made a life for himself. Instead of dwelling on the past, he had created his own future. He worked hard to ensure that future.

Mallory had thought she was working for her future, too, and in a small way, she had been, but she'd let the past hold her back.

Jack had been right to be angry with her the day before. She had spent months, more than two years, in fact, obsessing about finding Lying Jude's lost treasure and showing her ex-husband how wrong he was. All of his words would be thrown back in his face once she'd found it. Looking at it from Jack's point of view, though, showing up her ex-husband didn't really matter very much. It was true that she already had as many challenges as one person could possibly need.

Getting ahead with her life was what mattered, and she very much wanted Jack to be part of her life. How could she convince him of that, though, when she had spent weeks making sure that he knew she was independent and self-sufficient?

Could she convince him of her love for him when she'd demonstrated that she was still emotionally involved with Charles? She only hoped it wasn't too late. Tears came to her eyes and spilled over at the thought that he might not accept her love.

The sound of the door opening startled her. She threw the covers off her head and raised herself on her elbow, bringing up the sheet to cover herself with one hand and quickly swiping away her tears with the other.

Jack stopped with his hand on the doorknob. His head snapped up at the sudden movement in the bed, and his stricken gaze riveted on her. Emotions ran swiftly across his face—worry, then regret—then his eyes went blank as if he didn't want her to know what he was thinking.

He stepped inside and shut the door, but he didn't approach the bed. "Mallory, what's wrong?"

She tried to smile, but realized her lips were too shaky. "I was thinking about yesterday, about what you said, and about last night..."

He winced. "It's upset you."

"Well, yes."

"I'm sorry, Mallory."

Frantically trying to read his face, she said, "We'd better talk about it."

"No." He turned away. "I said I'm sorry. Get dressed. We'd better head back."

"You mean back into the mountains?"

"Home."

Confused, Mallory pulled herself to a sitting position. "Are the horses—"

"They're fine. Just spooked by a wild animal." Jack remained in the doorway. "It's time for us to go home, though."

Stunned, she gaped at him. Where was this coming from? Why was he apologizing and why was he suddenly so cold and withdrawn?

She couldn't let things end like this. If they went home, she would lose this chance. "I thought we were staying another day. We still have many places to search, and..."

It was the wrong thing to say. She knew it immediately when his face closed off and his eyes turned cold. "I know it's important to you, Mallory, but it'll have to be another time."

"It isn't that important to me, Jack." She started to rise from the bed, then recalled that she had nothing on. It wouldn't have bothered her if she had been facing the man with whom she had shared such intimacy the night before. But Jack seemed like a stranger now. She'd never seen him look like this, his face hard and distant.

Reaching out with one hand, she grasped the edge of the blanket and pulled it up around herself. Her eyes remained fixed on Jack and she saw hurt cross his face, then more coldness.

"I'll stay outside for a few minutes so you can get dressed."

Before she could call out to him, he stepped back and closed the door.

Something serious was going on here. Mallory intended to get to the bottom of it as fast as possible. She untangled herself from the various bed covers, scooped up her clothes, and hurried to the bathroom, where she quickly cleaned up and dressed. Unlike yesterday, she was grateful that Jack had made her leave her makeup behind. It meant she could get back to him more quickly. She ran a brush through her hair and hurried out.

He had made coffee and was standing by the counter sipping a cup as he looked out the window and watched the sun's rays spearing through the pines.

Mallory's heart plunged sickeningly when he didn't even turn around and look at her. Telling herself that if she stayed cool and calm, things could be worked out, she poured herself a cup of coffee. The hand holding the cup shook so badly the liquid sloshed to the rim. She supported it with her other hand.

After a fortifying sip, she said, "Jack, why don't you tell me what's wrong?"

He set his cup down and turned to her. His face was sober, pale and drawn.

"I've got to apologize for last night," he began, then stopped as if picking over his words.

Mallory blinked. "Last night?"

"Making love to you was a mistake."

Her mouth dropped open. She knew she was beginning to sound like an echo, but all she could do was repeat what he had said since it didn't seem to be able to register in her brain. "A mistake?"

His hand sliced the air impatiently. "It doesn't change anything, help anything."

"Change? Help?" she repeated, still trying to make sense of what he was saying.

"I thought it would, but I was wrong." He set his cup down in the sink and ran water into it. "There's nothing that can be done. Let's go home."

Shakily, Mallory set her own cup down. He didn't love her. She had only been fooling herself into thinking there was a chance he might. Still, she wasn't going to give up without a fight.

"A while ago you said you were sorry. Why? And why are you saying that making love to me was a mistake?"

His mouth was drawn into a firm line, his green eyes dark with pain. "Because I thought I could make you love me."

Now she really stared. She opened her mouth, closed it again, then opened it to blurt, "But I *do* love you."

He shifted away from her. "Mallory, don't say—"

She grabbed his arm so he would have to look at her. "I do love you."

"But you were crying when I came in this morning." He ran a hand through his hair. "Hell, I've never made a woman cry before."

"I thought I was going to have a hard time convincing you to love me." Hope sprang into his eyes and she laughed, a little sound of immense relief. "After yesterday, and what you said, I thought..." She shrugged. "I thought there was no chance that you would ever care about me."

"I would never have touched you if I didn't love you. In fact, I think I've loved you ever since you walked into that little shack of mine and demanded my attention."

"Jack," she said at a loss.

His arms opened and she stepped into them, feeling as if she had come home. His arms closed around her and his mouth found hers in a hard kiss.

"I love you," she said when he let her up for air. "I was afraid I'd really messed things up by being so obsessed with Lying Jude's bank money and trying to prove that I was right and Charles was wrong."

"We'll find that treasure someday," Jack assured her. "But somehow it just doesn't seem very important right now."

"You're right. Nothing is important enough to make me live in the past."

"It took you long enough to figure that out," he grumbled.

"You have to understand I didn't expect to meet someone like you—someone who wouldn't be scared off by my fears."

A tinge of red ran beneath his skin and he said, "Your fears didn't scare me. What scared me was that you wouldn't be willing to overcome them. That's why I . . ."

She pulled back, studying the uncomfortable look on his face. "You what?"

"I planted the map in the window seat."

"You *what*?"

He released her and stepped back, holding up his hands. "Now really, didn't it occur to you that it was a little too much of a coincidence that we found that map the night after you told me you had the journal?"

"The map isn't genuine?"

"Yes, it's genuine. George Early gave it to my grandfather—"

"Who gave it to your mother, who gave it to you."

"Yeah, but it never made much sense. I thought it might with the notations in the journal, but no one ever knew what had happened to George's journal."

"So when you found out I had it, you decided to plant the map and get me interested so you could get your hands on the journal?"

"Hell, no. I just wanted to get my hands on you. Or at least to get you alone so we could work things out. Then Charlie showed up, then you seemed so intent on the treasure, and—"

"And I almost blew it." She crossed her arms and gave him a resigned look. "I should be angry with you." She shook her head. "There you were, pretending to study that map like you'd never seen it before... I *really* ought to be angry with you!"

His eyes sparked with deviltry. "But how can you? You love me." He pulled her into his arms and kissed her again. "Marry me, Mallory. Marriage to me won't be a trap like your marriage to Charles."

"I know." She had never been more sure of anything in her life.

"Let's end the Clanton/Earp feud forever, shall we?"

She smiled. "At least our version of it."

He grinned. "A Clanton marrying an Earp. What would Wyatt, Virgil and Ike think?"

She smiled into his eyes. "They would think I'm the luckiest girl in the world."

Their wedding was held one month later in a small church in Tombstone. Only close family and friends attended. T.C. was best man and Sammi was maid of honor. Mallory's parents flew in from Africa for the wedding, taken aback by the sudden changes in both their daughters' lives.

The reception was open to all their family and friends, but Jack and Mallory were surprised by several uninvited guests—a number of reporters had shown up.

"Did you invite these people?" Mallory asked as Jack swept her into his arms for their first dance as husband and wife.

"No." He looked over her head as they twirled around the floor. Several photographers darted in and out among the crowd, trying to get good shots of the new Mr. and Mrs. Clanton. "Suppose I should have Fred and Jim Jackman help me throw them out?"

She lifted an eyebrow at him. "That would be the height of rudeness, even for you. What do you think they want?"

He grinned at her. "Are you kidding? They represent the Tombstone paper, the Bisbee paper, both major Arizona papers and two tabloids. They're getting the story of the year—the year 1881. An Earp marrying a Clanton."

He twirled her into an intricate series of steps and Mallory had to pause and gather up the train of her long white gown. "I can't believe that that many people would be interested in this."

"Honey, you'd be surprised." He scooped her into his arms again and looked down at her, the familiar devilish gleam in his eye. "It would probably blow their whole story if I told them the truth."

"The truth about what?"

He leaned close and whispered in her ear. "My family name's not really Clanton."

"What?"

"My father's father came over from Germany. His real name was Klinkmann. He wanted an American name, so he changed it to Clanton. Just picked it out of the phone book one day."

Mallory stared at him, then burst out laughing. "You're not even really related to Ike and Billy and that whole notorious bunch?"

"Not by so much as a drop of blood. It was just pure luck that my dad traveled through this area, liked it, and then married somebody with roots here."

She burst out laughing again as he twirled her around the floor. "You're a rat, do you know that?"

"I know."

"I think that's probably why you love me."

"I guess you're right."

Laughing together, they sailed through the dance, secure in their love and in their future.

Tombstone, Arizona was a good place for a wedding.

UNLOCK THE DOOR TO GREAT ROMANCE AT BRIDE'S BAY RESORT

Join Harlequin's new across-the-lines series, set in an exclusive hotel on an island off the coast of South Carolina.

Seven of your favorite authors will bring you exciting stories about fascinating heroes and heroines discovering love at Bride's Bay Resort.

Look for these fabulous stories coming to a store near you beginning in January 1996.

Harlequin American Romance #613 in January
Matchmaking Baby by Cathy Gillen Thacker

Harlequin Presents #1794 in February
Indiscretions by Robyn Donald

Harlequin Intrigue #362 in March
Love and Lies by Dawn Stewardson

Harlequin Romance #3404 in April
Make Believe Engagement by Day Leclaire

Harlequin Temptation #588 in May
Stranger in the Night by Roseanne Williams

Harlequin Superromance #695 in June
Married to a Stranger by Connie Bennett

Harlequin Historicals #324 in July
Dulcie's Gift by Ruth Langan

Visit Bride's Bay Resort each month wherever Harlequin books are sold.

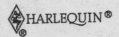

BBAYG

Yo amo novelas con corazón!

Starting this March, Harlequin opens up to a whole new world of readers with two new romance lines in SPANISH!

Harlequin Deseo
- passionate, sensual and exciting stories

Harlequin Bianca
- romances that are fun, fresh and very contemporary

With four titles a month, each line will offer the same wonderfully romantic stories that you've come to love—now available in Spanish.

Look for them at selected retail outlets.

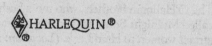

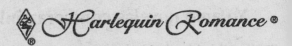

New from Harlequin Romance
a very special six-book series by

The town of Hard Luck, Alaska, needs women!

The O'Halloran brothers, who run a bush-plane service
called Midnight Sons, are heading a campaign to
attract women to Hard Luck. (*Location: north of the
Arctic Circle. Population: 150—mostly men!*)

"Debbie Macomber's *Midnight Sons* series is a delightful
romantic saga. And each book is a powerful, engaging story
in its own right. Unforgettable!"
                                        —Linda Lael Miller

TITLE IN THE MIDNIGHT SONS SERIES: